'If you aren't reading B P Walter yet, now's the time'
A. J. Finn

'I will read anything B P Walter writes'
Gillian McAllister

'Unpredictable, whip smart, utterly absorbing'
John Marrs

'One of the most unsettling novels of recent years. It's also one of the most compelling'
John Boyne

'Searing, sinister and addictive'
Chris Whitaker

'Strong shades of Patricia Highsmith'
Lisa Hall

'A sinister slow-burn about the darkest human desires'
Charlotte Duckworth

'Kept me entirely hooked…'
Alice Clark-Platts

B P Walter was born and raised in Essex. After spending his childhood and teenage years reading compulsively, he worked in bookshops then went to the University of Southampton to study Film and English followed by an MA in Film & Cultural Management. He is an alumnus of the Faber Academy and formerly worked in social media coordination for Waterstones in London.

X x.com/barnabywalter
f facebook.com/BPWalterAuthor
instagram.com/bpwalterauthor

Also by B P Walter

A Version of the Truth

Hold Your Breath

The Dinner Guest

The Woman on the Pier

The Locked Attic

Notes on a Murder

THE GARDEN PARTY

B P WALTER

One More Chapter
a division of HarperCollins*Publishers*
1 London Bridge Street
London SE1 9GF
www.harpercollins.co.uk
HarperCollins*Publishers*
Macken House, 39/40 Mayor Street Upper,
Dublin 1, D01 C9W8, Ireland

1

This paperback edition 2024
First published in Great Britain by
HarperCollins*Publishers* 2024

This novel is entirely a work of fiction. The names, characters and
incidents portrayed in it are the work of the author's imagination.
Any resemblance to actual persons, living or dead, events or localities
is entirely coincidental.

Playlist

In Full Bloom - Clint Mansell ♥

Piano Trio No. 2, op. 100 - Franz Schubert ♥

Sunrise Prelude - Daft Punk ♥

Les jumeaux miroirs - Philippe Rombi ♥

Dead Things - Philip Glass ♥

Wrecking Ball - Midnite String Quartet ♥

Serenade In G Major: Eine Kleine Nachtmusik, K. 525: IV. Rondo: Allegro - Wolfgang Amadeus Mozart, The English Concert

Hitting the Fan - David Buckley ♥

Duet - Sugar Vendil & Trevor Gureckis ♥

The Departure - Max Richter, Lang Lang ♥

Charms - Abel Korzeniowski ♥

Toxic - Aramis String Quartet ♥

Une amitié - Philippe Rombi ♥

For my family

All happy families are alike; each unhappy family is unhappy in its own way.

— Leo Tolstoy, *Anna Karenina*

One day you will do things for me that you hate. That is what it means to be family.

— Jonathan Safran Foer, *Everything is Illuminated*

Prologue

It isn't clear who lets out the scream. But once it has sounded, a second follows swiftly afterwards from another direction.

There is a pause. A moment when the scales between order and chaos are juddering, shifting, then eventually spill over. Chaos reigns.

Guests leap from their seats and dash over to the top table where the Moncrieffs are sitting. Patrick is slumped forwards, unmoving.

The bride-to-be is shaking her fiancé, trying to get him to respond. But his blank eyes stare out. No speech comes from his lips. Her parents have come round the front of the table. Have joined their daughter in trying to get some sense out of their future son-in-law.

An elderly relative has reached the main table and

has two fingers pressed against one of their necks, checking for a pulse. Waiting.

'Phone an ambulance!' someone shouts.

'I have, they're on the way,' says another.

'Give them space, give them some air,' another cries.

The old man says in a panicked tone, 'I can't find a pulse. I can't find a pulse.'

'Oh, my God,' cries another.

'They're dead!'

'Someone just said they're all dead.'

'Seriously?'

'Yes, all of them. Someone's checked the pulses.'

'I think one of them might be alive, I can't be sure.'

'Apparently nobody can find a pulse.'

'What's happening?'

As the guests crowd and shout and cast around for something to do or something to say, nobody notices two young men striding across the lawn in the bright late-spring sunshine, then head around the side of the house. Away from the tent. Away from the party. Before long, both are out of sight, away from the chaos unfolding in the garden. Never to return.

Part I

THE CRIMES OF RAPHAEL MONCRIEFF

Chapter One

HARRIS

Two months before the party

The sun was streaming harsh and hot through Harris's bedroom the morning he got the invitation. He somehow knew, as soon as he opened his eyes, that it would be a difficult day. Any day in spring that started so uncomfortably stifling couldn't go well, he thought as he pulled himself out of bed, picking up a water bottle off the floor. He drank deeply, feeling dehydrated. Maybe he'd had too much of the wine the night before. He never normally drank on nights before he had a full day of lectures. He was usually disciplined. Didn't find it hard to stick to his habits of calm moderation. But this had been a tricky week. Difficult decisions. A lot to think about. And there were times when the thought of what was to come did play on his mind.

After downing the rest of the water, he wandered through into the main living area of the flat and over to Rhys's bedroom door. From the start of them living together shortly after the beginning of Harris's first semester in London, they'd never once knocked before entering each other's rooms; just walked in, as if such niceties and overtures were for more formal, more reserved people than them. This sense of instant familiarity and closeness had taken Harris by surprise. He'd never thought he would feel this connected to someone. It was as if he had spent the first part of his life as someone adrift, believing himself separate from everyone, convinced that would continue until he was old and ready to die. But then Rhys had entered his life and everything changed. Living together had been a dream. Or at least it had until Rhys had started bringing girls home. It had started with a few one-night stands here and there, and Harris didn't mind, so long as they arrived in the evening and left early the next morning. But one of the girls, Ivanka, someone he'd stayed in touch with from his previous flatshare, had started visiting a couple of times a week. And she'd linger during the day, too, 'hanging out' with Rhys on the sofa, watching TV or sharing takeaways. Harris couldn't help but feel annoyed. Jealous, even. And, at times, embarrassed, when the not-bothering-to-knock thing led to awkward interruptions.

'Hey, man, not a good moment,' Rhys called out that morning when Harris walked into his room, rushing to pull the duvet over their bodies.

'Oh, shit, sorry,' Harris said, 'I didn't know she was still here.'

'*She* has a name,' said the girl's voice from the bed. 'Good morning, *Harris*.' In her cutting, Russian-accented tone, she made the word 'Harris' sound like an insult.

'Sorry, Ivanka,' Harris muttered as he exited.

While Rhys and his sort-of-girlfriend finished their morning activities, Harris busied himself making breakfast. He'd only just pulled down the lever of the toaster when he heard the door open and Rhys came ambling out of his room in his boxers, running a hand through his dishevelled hair.

'Ivanka's pissed,' he said, coming to a stop in front of the kitchen counter, biting his lip.

'Back on the drink, is she,' Harris muttered.

'No, pissed, as in, *pissed off*.'

Harris said nothing.

'She thinks you find her annoying and ... well, that you treat her as a nuisance.'

Harris sighed. 'Do you want some toast?'

'You're evading,' Rhys said, with something between a tut and a laugh, going round the kitchen island and taking down his protein shake powder from one of the top cupboards.

'I'm not sure they're working,' Harris said, nodding at the shake, 'you're still as skinny as ever.'

Rhys grunted a laugh back. 'The bulk will come,' he said. 'Oh, did you see that came for you?' He nodded at the kitchen table.

On its surface was a cream envelope with an ornate, violet border. Harris knew what it was straight away. But still, he had to open it, even if it meant tearing it up afterwards, or burning it on the stove and watching its lavender-scented pages curl.

The invitation wasn't lavender-scented, after all, or at least he got no hint of it as he pealed open the envelope and pulled out the short card inside, which summed up his role in that family: sort-of-part-of-them but not quite. Perhaps Raphael and Lauren felt they were being kind by sending him an invite, but Harris saw it almost as another act of distancing. He was a guest. An outsider. Not a member of the family you just presumed would be there. He had to be *invited*, like a friend or a relation outside of the close-knit unit.

He scanned over the text on the card. Keywords jumping out at him.

Invite you.

A party to celebrate the engagement.

A joyous occasion.

Would it be, though? Harris thought. Would it really

be a *joyous occasion*? More a hastily-organised, borderline-desperate attempt to claw back some respectability. But, in spite of his many feelings about the Moncrieff family, he was surprised to feel a stab of jealousy. There would be people at the gathering who genuinely wished the young couple well, who'd be delighted they were getting married and setting off on a life of apparent married bliss. Nobody would ever feel that way about him, he thought. That sort of collective celebration wasn't part of his world.

'Perhaps I should be flattered I'm invited,' Harris said, trying to keep his voice steady.

Rhys didn't say anything, but was watching him closely.

'I think,' said Harris, setting down his shake and folding his arms, 'it's time to iron out the details of our plan.'

Rhys nodded. 'You're sure you still want to go through with it?'

Harris nodded. He thought of Isabella and Patrick, the perfect parents on the outside, their charming son Raphael marrying his beautiful bride. Thinking about them smiling and laughing in the grounds of the family home made him clench his hands. 'Yes. And after everything that's happened – everything we've found out – I don't think we're going far enough. And as I said, they're not going to have a big reception, due to the pregnancy. It's just going to be the service for the vows, then they'll be off on their honeymoon. It won't be public enough.' He went over to the fridge and used one of the round, black magnets to hold the invite in place. He re-read it, then said quietly, 'Let's bring things forward. This engagement party is in lieu of a big reception. Let's do it then.'

Chapter Two

HARRIS

The day of the party

On the day he brings his world tumbling down, Harris wakes with a jolt at 3am. The faces of his adopted family hovering in the front of his mind. For a moment, amidst the disorientation and darkness, he thinks they are there with him, standing around his bed, watching him. But as he sits up and reaches for his glass of water, he knows this is just a trick of the mind. He knows within seconds of waking and sitting upright that he has been dreaming, but it still unnerves him. It's like he's being haunted. Haunted by ghosts of people who were still alive. Alive for the moment, at least. He feels annoyed at himself for feeling so het up, for being at the mercy of his subconscious. He had tried to have as calm an evening as possible the night before in an attempt to stop himself going over detail after detail of what might be said, what might happen, where things might lead. He'd had a hot bath, had gone to bed early and listened to a podcast about volcanos, followed by some music – Largo from 'Winter' in Vivaldi's *The Four Seasons*, played by Yo-Yo Ma. The music soothed him enough so that sleep was possible. For a time, at least.

At 5.40am he gives up on sleep and dresses himself slowly, taking time to pull on each item, chosen in advance. Beige trousers, a navy-blue blazer and a pink shirt. His family will approve. It will probably be the only thing they'll approve of that day, he thinks to himself.

After a quick tidy of his hair in the bathroom – it never needs much, he's kept it fairly short since he was sixteen – he walks towards Rhys's room. Just before he reaches for the handle, he pauses, and isn't entirely sure why. He takes a deep breath. Swallows. He wonders if Rhys had experienced a similar disturbed night. Or if he'd slept soundly, peaceful in his ignorance about what turn the day ahead would take. Rhys would never forgive him if he knew. The lies. The betrayal. But the years since his parents died have made Harris like this. Made him ruthless, hard, calculating. He knows he needs to look out for himself above all others. He knows he's still alone in the world, no matter what anyone says.

When he finally goes inside the room, he finds Rhys staring out the window. He's pleased he's alone today.

No sign of Ivanka tangled in his sheets. Pleased it's just the two of them, for what might be the last time. Depending on how things went, of course. Rhys has a floor-to-ceiling window with a blind that is rarely pulled down, offering a dazzling view across Southwark, the river and the London eye visible to the left, although Harris had never seen him staring out of it before. Not like this, standing stationary, watching the dawn. Nor has he seen so clearly the look of uncertainty in Rhys's face before. But it is there, as he turns round to look at Harris, the pale sun making the dark skin of his face shimmer and glow.

'Nervous?' Harris asks, walking further into the room.

'A bit,' says Rhys, as through the window, the morning sun has started to shine through the gaps between the houses and apartment blocks.

'By this time tomorrow it will be done,' Harris says, taking a seat on the unmade bed. Rhys never makes it, not properly – something that would have driven Harris mad if they had been sharing a room.

'Did you want to go through the files one more time?' he asks.

'No,' says Harris, 'I went through the slides yesterday. I'm happy with everything.'

Rhys looks at him. 'Are you sure you want to keep everything in there. Like ... everything?'

Harris nods. 'Everything.'

Rhys says nothing for a moment, chewing his lip. Then says, 'You don't have to do it, you know.'

Harris doesn't acknowledge this. They remain in silence for a while, then eventually Harris says 'You ought to get ready. We should leave soon if we're going to get to Bath in good time.'

'Yeah,' Rhys says. He steps back from the window, and Harris gets the feeling he is dragging himself away from thoughts deeper and more complicated than he is letting on. They both have a lot on their minds, that's unavoidable. Today will send ripples through their lives. Perhaps not ripples, tidal waves, smashing through their sense of the day-to-day. Rhys has a sense of this, Harris can tell, but at least he doesn't know the full plan. If he did, Harris would be on his own.

'I'm going to have a quick shower,' Rhys says. 'I'll bring my uniform and will change when we arrive. I don't want to drive in it.'

Harris nods, offering a smile. Rhys sort-of returns it, but it's more like a jerk of his mouth than anything else. He goes to grab a cereal bar from the kitchen and Harris hopes to himself that it's just nerves that are making Rhys distant. He'd better not back out now. Not when they've come so far.

The drive to Bowen Hall in Bath goes smoothly, with the M4 surprisingly light and the weather remaining bright and dry. But on the last stretch of their journey, barely five miles from their destination, the police stop them. Rhys had realised he was in the wrong lane at a roundabout, changed lanes without indicating, then went round twice while he and Harris argued about which exit they needed to take. Harris grappled with a nonsensical sat-nav app on his phone trying to get it to show or repeat the necessary turn-off instruction, but in the end Rhys gave up and picked one at random, unable to glean the necessary information from the road signs surrounding them. All this is noticed by a police car, which follows them onto the quiet road Rhys's KA has turned into and signals them to pull over.

'Fuck. Oh fuck,' says Rhys, running his hand over his forehead.

'There's nothing to worry about,' Harris says, trying to convince himself this is true, watching in the rear-view mirror as the police officer gets out of his car and starts to walk over to them. 'You weren't speeding. Just tell him we're lost. Tell him the truth.'

'Shit,' Rhys says, gripping the steering wheel tightly.

The police officer, when he arrives at the window and gestures for it to be lowered, is surprisingly polite, friendly even, apparently 'just checking everything was okay' as he'd noticed the boys had 'gone round the roundabout a few times more than one would expect'.

He had also noticed the lane drifting. In spite of his kind manner, however, Harris is worried how stressed he and Rhys must look, with Rhys's hands trembling as he is breathalysed (and tests negative for any alcohol). Afterwards, once they are on their way again, Rhys still seems upset, his hands continuing to shake.

'Are you okay?' Harris asks. 'Did you really think that cop was going to arrest you?'

Rhys doesn't answer for a moment. Then he says, 'Don't you feel it was a bad omen?'

'Omen? No. I don't believe in omens or superstitions or any of that shit.'

'My mum did,' Rhys says quietly.

Harris doesn't know what to say to this, so closes his mouth and thinks for a bit. Then says, 'We're doing this for your mum. And for mine. And for everything else that family has done.'

'I know,' Rhys says, nodding.

'So just … keep calm.'

'I will,' says Rhys, still nodding, pulling down the sun visor to block out the bright, late-morning sunshine, 'and anyway, we're not doing anything illegal, of course. I just … I don't know… I find the whole social shaming thing a bit stressful.'

Rhys is driving smoothly again, but his knuckles are still white on the wheel. *Nothing illegal*, Harris thinks to himself as they lapse into silence. If only that were true.

Chapter Three

RAPHAEL

The day of the party

Raphael Moncrieff wakes up on the day of his engagement party with a sense of dread hanging heavy around him. He turns over to feel the cold side of the pillow next to him, enjoying having the space to stretch out. Whenever he shared a bed with his fiancé, he couldn't help but feel cramped and uncomfortable, especially in the queen-size bed in her Oxford flat. There wasn't enough room for his long legs and, more than once, he'd accidentally kicked or knocked Lauren in the night, waking her up with a start, then had to apologise and try to go back to sleep. Instead of suggesting they sleep in a bigger bed, though, she often seemed to find this more amusing than annoying, joking about it the next morning and saying how she loved how close and 'intertwined' they were. He particularly dislikes that word, *intertwined*. It makes him feel like his relationship is a creeper plant, like the Devil's Snare in *Harry Potter*, locking him into place, restricting his freedoms, shutting down his options.

And his options *were* shut down. He was to marry Lauren Rizzini because that is what his parents desired. When they discovered their son had gotten Lauren pregnant during his final year at university, his mother had gone completely white and looked as if she would faint, and his father had smashed a bone china plate against a wall. 'How could you have been so stupid?' Isabella had asked, putting her head in her hands, before turning to her husband and saying 'And that better be the last plate you fling at the wall. We're not that sort of family.'

Patrick had let out a laugh at that. 'Apparently we are. Full-blown *EastEnders* here, with Raphael unable to figure out how condoms work.' The comparison had been an apt one, and for a moment during that confrontation, Raphael had felt as though he'd slipped into a play, or even a TV soap of the kind his mother pretended not to watch (he'd once seen the 'iPlayer downloads' section of her iPad, so he knew the full truth). The explosive reaction from his parents only got worse when they picked over all the 'issues' with the situation. Although they had met Lauren and seemed to like her, they took the opportunity to find new faults with her – the fact she was less 'girl' and more 'older woman', since she was twenty-eight, a full seven years older than him (a PhD student, in the midst of her doctorate on Georgian Literature). To further aggravate the matter, he'd revealed to his parents, who at that point were convinced the situation couldn't get any worse, that the woman had, as part of her PhD, been doing some seminar tutoring and he was one of the students in her class. This was a detail he hadn't originally revealed to his mother or father, but upon the revelation of the pregnancy, he wished he'd been up-front from the start.

'So you've been fucking your tutor?' his dad had said, spitting out his words, his face uncharacteristically red, eyes so intense Raphael wondered if they might melt.

'She's not really my tutor...' Raphael had said, trying to fight off the urge to both cry and start smashing crockery himself.

'As good as,' his mother had replied, getting up from the table and stepping over the fragments of broken plate on the floor on her way through to the kitchen.

It had been a thoroughly miserable affair and Raphael had gone to bed that night without saying anything to either of his parents. Lauren had phoned later that evening to ask 'how it had all gone'. Raphael hadn't sugarcoated things. 'Imagine an absolute fucking awful shitshow, then times it by three thousand.'

'Oh, Raphy, try not to worry,' Lauren said, using a nickname he hated. Its use was exclusive to her and the fact that nobody ever called him that had either not occurred to her or she perhaps found it endearing she had her own pet name for him. It was the kind of thing she'd found sweet.

'Of course I'm bloody worried,' he said, 'If they cut me off I—'

'I'm no gold digger, Raphy. You could be as poor as one of those unfortunates you see in documentaries and I would still love you.'

'Well ... that's all very lovely, but ... I kind of care. A lot, actually. It wouldn't be fair. It's the unfairness of it all.'

'Of course it is, I know the money's nothing to you, too, and it isn't important—'

'The money *is* important, that's what I'm bloody saying.'

'Don't get snappy, it's all going to be fine,' she said, clearly trying to sound soothing.

'I've got to go,' he said, 'I need to sleep.'

'Goodnight my dearest, I hope you get some rest and...'

He'd cut the call.

The next day, it was all change. His parents had convened for an emergency summit while he'd been asleep. And they had a plan.

'You'll marry her,' Patrick had told his son firmly. 'We'll have some details to iron out. But yes, the plan is that you'll have to marry her.'

'You are aware of the year, aren't you?' Raphael had said. 'You do know this is the twenty-first century, not the nineteenth?'

'The wedding will need to be soon,' Isabelle added, ignoring him, 'May or June, I think, before it's obvious she's pregnant. Providing she's told you the truth about dates and such.'

'Of course she's told me the truth,' Raphael said. 'Don't imply that again, it's not nice. But ... what if I don't want to get married? I'm twenty-one.'

'What you want,' Patrick said, slowly, his harsh, dark eyes burning into him, 'is irrelevant.' He then raised an eyebrow. 'Unless, of course, you want to go your own way with all this.'

The meaning was clear. Play the game, do as you're told, or you're on your own.

So he played the game. He proposed to Lauren a week later in her Oxford apartment when she arrived home with one arm full of dusty hardback books and the other holding a bag of supermarket shopping. She immediately said yes, proclaimed that day the best of her life so far, and they celebrated by eating a Waitrose Very Best Dine In for two Truffle Chicken Kiev. Afterwards, they sat on her uncomfortable grey sofa watching a DVD of the 2007 adaptation of *Persuasion*, with Lauren giving an unbroken running commentary on how it compared with the original text, and Raphael sitting completely still wondering how his life had gone so spectacularly wrong.

He didn't dislike Lauren. He actually quite liked her in some respects. And in many ways, she fitted. She was beautiful, intelligent, upper-middle-class, if not exactly rich. But the pregnancy had accelerated things, made things move quicker than he would have wanted and he'd felt manoeuvred and manipulated – not by her, exactly, but by those around him. His parents, and to some extent hers, too. And he couldn't help sometimes taking out his frustration and resentment on her.

As the weeks passed, his fiancé bought things in large quantities in preparation for both wedding and baby and liaised with Isabelle and the event planner for the engagement party. Raphael was curious to note how the two women managed to get on perfectly well, with his mother remaining blunt and borderline unfriendly, and Lauren being her usual jolly self, apparently unphased by Isabelle's demeanour and tone. Raphael met Lauren's parents (her father was a producer at the BBC, her mother was a Harley Street doctor's receptionist) and did his best to appear jovial and excited for the wedding, all the while trying to hide his sweating palms and juddering legs – a nervous habit of his when he was under stress or anxious. The wedding would be a very small, discreet affair, it was decided, with an engagement party held a little while before it in place of a grand reception. The story would be that they wanted the day itself to be 'fuss-free' to make it possible to enjoy their love for each other without distractions.

Now the day of the engagement party is upon him and Raphael is shocked to find the whole thing is actually happening. He's become used to telling himself it's all some elaborate hoax or a dream that he will soon wake up from, or that someone would shout 'fooled you!' and then reveal Lauren as a trained actor, the whole thing part of an edgy reality TV show. But of course, no such thing has occurred. Now he must face the party after a night of broken sleep. He is in the process of heaving himself out of bed when the door opens and both his parents walk in.

'Good, you're awake, we got tired of waiting,' his mother says in a business-like tone, walking over to the curtains and flinging them open.

'Hurry up and get dressed,' his father says, 'we need you to help with the chair fiasco.'

'It's not a fucking fiasco,' Isabelle snaps at him.

'That's *your* word. You said it was a *fiasco* not half an hour ago.'

'Fine,' she concedes to her husband, 'it is a fiasco. I just knew something would go wrong today.'

'Christ, can you both leave?' Raphael says, frozen to the spot. Drama like this from his parents is the last thing he needs today. 'I could do without this now.'

'I'm sorry it's not convenient, but these things matter,' his mother says, icily. 'I gave birth to you. They literally quarried you out of me, it hasn't been the same down there since, so forgive me if I want to oversee every detail of my precious son's important day.'

'*Engineered* important day,' Raphael mutters.

'We wanted to reiterate what we said yesterday about Great Aunt Elizabeth,' Patrick says.

'I know, I know,' groaned Raphael. 'You literally said it twelve hours ago – don't let on Lauren's pregnant, don't let on you're cohabiting. I thought all that was supposed to be secret, anyway? At least the first part. I'm hardly about to start advertising it to the most intolerant and Catholic member of the family.'

'We wanted to remind you. You've slept since then, and you have a history of insensitivity and lack of tact when it comes to Elizabeth. And she has an unfortunate habit of keeling over with heart attacks. I would prefer to avoid any such drama today.'

'Can you please just leave,' he says, firmly.

'We need you showered, dressed and downstairs in five minutes,' Patrick says, turning to go.

'Make that two,' Isabelle adds as they walk back out of the door, neither of them bothering to close it.

Instead of doing as he was told, Raphael collapsed back onto his bed with a half-sigh, half-moan, his hands over his eyes, as if by blocking out the light he could bring back the darkness of the night, rewind time, return to another day, another month, another year. There he lies, until a minute later his phone rings. With effort, he reaches over and answers.

'Hey Raphy,' Lauren says, her cheery voice as painful as knives on bare flesh. 'Are you getting ready? The weather is *perfect*. Do you know, if I believed in omens – well, I sort of do, of course – I would say this is a good one. My parents and I are leaving Oxford at ten, so should arrive at yours at noon.'

'I know,' Raphael murmurs.

'Gosh, I'm excited,' she says breathlessly. 'This will be a day we'll never forget, my love.'

Chapter Four

HARRIS

The day of the party

Harris and Rhys part ways shortly before they get to the driveway of Bowen Hall. They stop on a deserted country road about five minutes away so Rhys can change into his caterer's uniform of tight, black, skinny suit trousers, white shirt and black tie. Harris stays in the car while he gets out to slip his clothes on. Rhys had flatly refused to get changed in the gents of a service station, saying he'd probably catch something or ruin his shirt. Harris told him he had more chance getting mud on his shirt changing at the side of the road in the countryside, but it didn't seem to make a difference. Once dressed, they drive down the last few roads until they got near the entrance to the estate.

'You should get out here,' Harris says. 'Then make

your way up the drive on foot. That way it can be like you've been dropped off by someone. I'll park the car outside the front of the house.'

Rhys nods and gets out. Harris notices his eyes look red and strained and darting about him. 'You sure you're okay?' he asks.

'Fine,' Rhys says, 'I'll … well, I guess I'll see you in there. I'll let you know how it's … how it's all going. If I can.'

'I'll keep my phone on, so you can always message if you can't talk to me,' Harris says.

'And if I can't … if there's no way to do it without someone—'

'I'll press ahead regardless,' says Harris. 'The … um … visuals will be an added extra. But the real impact will be in what I'm going to say. And once I've said it, there'll be no taking it back.'

Rhys nods and leaves. Harris drives through the already open gates up the driveway he knows so well. The frontage, featuring a two-storey colonnade of Corinthian columns styled in white, like the rest of the building, comes instantly into view.

He parks outside the front of the house, finding the clutch on Rhys's KA difficult and unpredictable, and almost grazes the side on the neat stone wall that separates the driveway from the front lawn.

The front door is opened by Isabelle Moncrieff herself

– a surprise to Harris, as this is a job normally left to the housekeeper, Emmeline.

'Oh, you're here,' Isabelle says, which was about as friendly as she's ever been to him. 'Good. You can go and hurry up Raphael.'

'Where's Emmeline,' Harris asks, stepping inside.

'Sorting out the chair fiasco,' Isabelle says. 'There's been a terrible mix-up – they've sent the wrong sort of—'

She stops suddenly in the middle of closing the door, then peers out of it before turning to Harris with a look of horror and disgust on her face. 'What on earth is *that*?'

'What?'

'That car!' she says, pointing to Rhys's battered and dirt-flecked KA.

'It's what I came in. I borrowed it. Off a friend.'

'Well it can't stay there,' she says, looking at Harris as though he was insane, 'it looks hideous.'

'I thought that was where—'

'Get it out of sight, now. There should be space in one of the garages. Or in the bushes over there,' she gestures vaguely to a shaded area of trees and foliage to the left side of the house.

There was a time when Harris would have done as he was told, just to keep the peace. But today isn't like any other day. Today, things are going to change. 'I think it's fine,' he says, folding his arms. Isabelle gapes at him. For the next few seconds they remain in a stand-off. Then at last she says 'Fine, leave the keys on the side and I'll get someone to move it.'

Amused that she clearly wouldn't dream of sullying herself by driving the vehicle herself, Harris tosses the keys onto the gleaming varnished side table, not caring if they scuff the surface, and begins to march up the stairs in the direction of Raphael's room.

He goes across the warmly lit landing and down a corridor. He's never got used to the Moncrieff's habit of leaving all the lights on in practically every room all the time, even in the daytime. Perhaps it's their way of making it clear they had money to burn, he thinks to himself. Or that environmental consideration isn't something that enters their orbit.

Harris knocks on the bedroom door and receives a 'Come in,' in a monotone as a reply. Inside, he finds Raphael sitting on the window seat in his room, his eyes cast down at the floor. He is in a smart shirt but no trousers, sitting on the edge of the seat in his boxer shorts, holding two ties in his hands, as if the decision of choosing which to wear has become too much for him.

'Cheer up,' Harris greets him. 'It's not your wedding day. Just the engagement party.'

Raphael barely looks at him, just shrugs and then swaps the ties over in his hand, perhaps hoping that would help him see them in a new light. 'Well this is the big event, isn't it?' he mutters. 'The big circus. One of the best days of our lives, or so Lauren keeps telling me.'

'And you don't believe her?' asks Harris, lightly.

Another shrug. 'I suppose.' He looks at the ties again, then lifts his head and asks, 'Did my mum send you?' Always *my* mum, Harris notes. Never just 'Mum'.

'Sort of,' Harris replies, 'she seems stressed.'

'Something about chairs,' Raphael mumbles. Then, with a grunt, pulls himself up, cracking his knuckles and looking at Harris square-on. 'Why did you come? I thought you and my dad had a row or something? He said he didn't think you'd turn up.'

Harris shrugs. 'Well, I stayed for Christmas. I didn't storm out then, I just didn't speak to him and he didn't speak to me. So if I can survive that, I'm sure I can get through today.'

'What was the row about? When was it? He wouldn't properly discuss it.'

Harris shook his head. 'Just things. It was when he picked me up from uni for Christmas break. It was a few months ago. More, even. I don't want to go into it.'

Raphael nods slowly, although it's clear he doesn't understand. 'Well ... it's good you're here today, I suppose.'

For a moment, Harris contemplates saying something mysterious, something to just put the cat among his already unsettled pigeons. But he decides now isn't the right time, and he has Rhys's voice in his head, telling him to stick to the plan. So instead of making any dark hints or veiled references, he decides to keep it simple. 'I'm here for you.'

He doesn't mean these words. Now he knows what Raphael has been up to – what he's done – Harris has no intention of offering him actual support. Quite the opposite. But for now, he decides to string things out a bit further. Bide his time.

Raphael's expression softens. For a moment, Harris could have sworn he sees his lower lip tremble, as if he's about to cry. Then Raphael tosses the ties aside and pulls Harris into an awkward hug.

'Thanks. I … well, thanks. I realise we haven't had time to talk … the whole engagement has rather taken up my time and … the other thing.'

'The pregnancy.'

Raphael's face instantly closes up, as if a light has gone out inside.

'Yeah,' he says. 'That.'

A few beats of silence pass, then Harris says 'I emailed you. The essay. Did you see it?'

For a moment Raphael looked confused, then he nods, 'Oh, yes. Thanks. Really appreciate you doing that for me after all this time. I just knew it needed your magic touch.' He walks over to the bed and picks up the trousers laid out on it and begins to pull them on. 'I need to read through it properly, but I'm sure it will be another First. Couldn't have done it without you.'

That's true, Harris thinks to himself. He'd taken care

of the university essay, making sure it was up to the standard he would hope for his own work, knowing it would be the last he would ever do for Raphael.

'You should have come to Oxford,' Raphael said.

Harris shakes his head. 'I wanted to be in London.'

'Don't understand it,' Raphael says, 'but Lauren's been on about having a London home at some point, so I suppose we'll end up there.'

'Great. And the blue one.' Harris points to one of the tie options.

'Thanks,' Raphael says, picking it up and looping it round his neck. 'I was afraid I would have to ask Mum's opinion, and she's not best pleased with me right now. Wanted me downstairs ages ago.'

Once he's finished tying it, he comes over and lays a hand on Harris's shoulder. 'You're a pal.' He nods, jaw clenched, as if he's said something profound.

Harris thinks of all the things he could say in response. Things that would chill Raphael to the core. Things that were currently saved to a USB stick in Rhys's possession downstairs as he puts the first part of their plan into operation. But he doesn't. As they leave the room together, he decides to stay silent. For now.

Chapter Five

HARRIS

Three-and-a-half years before the party

Harris was asleep on the sofa when the car arrived. He had initially been sleeping in his school friend Aiden's bed, whilst Aiden slept on the sofa, but after the first night of next-to-no sleep, he'd gone downstairs at 5am to tell Aiden he could have his bed back. He might as well sleep on the sofa. So Aiden had gratefully loped upstairs, dragging his duvet, and Harris had settled on the sofa with the brand-new Sainsbury's duvet Aiden's mum had bought him the day he came.

Nobody in the family knew how to treat him. What do you say to a fifteen-year-old boy who has just lost both his parents? There are only so many times someone can say, 'I'm so sorry' or 'Are you okay?' The Swallow family had taken him in at the drop of a hat. Mary

Swallow had scooped him up like a fallen bird and eagerly welcomed him into her nest. Her husband, Mike Swallow, had been welcoming if somewhat awkward, patting him on the shoulder and saying 'You'll pull through, lad,' before shuffling off to watch *Traffic Cops*.

Aiden's response to his friend's family tragedy had been to start offering him his belongings. 'Would you like this pack of cards?' he'd say, picking up a wodge of dog-eared cardboard that had seen better days, or saying that when Harris went he could take a spare Blu-ray player as Aiden now used the one built into his games console. Harris had quietly declined these offers. After all, he had a lot of stuff already. A whole house full of things. Things he had no idea what to do with. All his mum's clothes. She had a lot of clothes. All his dad's football memorabilia. He had no interest in West Ham or who had signed what shirt. But he was told not to worry about all this. It would all be sorted.

The days and weeks folded into each other. Grown-ups had meetings, sometimes with him, sometimes without him. Officials, caseworkers, a lawyer named Mr Booth – all of them seated around Mary and Mike's kitchen table laying out documents or politely sipping weak tea whilst perched on the sofa and mentioning phrases like 'responsibility of the courts', 'lack of relations', 'custody' and 'parents' wishes'. They sometimes referred to his parents by their names, Erin and John, or Mr and Mrs Strong, or simply as 'the deceased'. The name 'Moncrieff' was mentioned sometimes and that 'the family had been contacted'. Harris didn't pay much attention. He knew he should, but he felt like he'd become an item – like a suitcase at an airport without an owner.

Grief had twisted itself around him, hard to define, even harder to escape. He cried sometimes in the downstairs loo when everyone was upstairs. He thought about how his parents had died when he was at school. He felt guilty their hearts had stopped during a horrific car accident while he'd carried on in his maths lesson at school, blissfully unaware. And when he thought about all of this he felt his hands start to tremble and the tears begin to fall. He ate, too. For the few days after learning of his parents' car crash, he didn't eat a thing. Didn't feel like it. Then his hunger returned. With an astonishing vengeance. It was like a force hitting him, that hunger. Like a searing itch in a wound that could never be properly scratched. He'd wait until the family slept and then he'd raid the fridge. Mary kept it constantly well-stocked so she either didn't notice or over-compensated when out shopping to make up for it. He'd sandwich great wedges of cheddar cheese between thick slices of heavily buttered bread and cram them into his mouth, then make another, and another. Then he'd start on the biscuits and the cookies and the doughnuts or leftover apple pie, finishing up with handfuls of Minstrels or

Celebrations or whatever else he could find in the cupboards. This was on top of the extremely generous portion sizes Mary served him and her husband and son every day for meals.

Part of him knew all this probably wasn't the healthiest way of dealing with his grief. But he didn't really know how to process it any other way. The sense of confusion and loss was like a drug, anaesthetising everyday life until his very thoughts and feelings became a blur. So when the car arrived outside the Swallow's house and a suited man got out, he hardly knew how long it had been since that first night when he'd made his way downstairs to the sofa in their front room.

'Harris, darling,' Mary had said, wringing her hands as she came over to him. 'I know it's early, but Patrick – Mr Moncrieff – is here.'

Harris rubbed his eyes and pulled himself up. 'Okay,' he said. He vaguely reached for his hair – he could feel it was sticking up. Mary perhaps knew what he was thinking and said, 'Why don't you just say hello, then you can shower and dress and I'll give him a cup of tea in the meantime.'

So he did as Mary suggested, shaking hands with the tall, suited man in the hallway, then climbing the stairs to get ready. He came down fifteen minutes later. He felt uncomfortable. His hands were cold but his T-shirt felt tight, which made him feel hot and prickly. He'd steadily become aware he'd put on weight since moving into the

Swallow's home and clothes that once sat comfortably on him now clung to his body.

The visitor was in conversation with Mary at the kitchen table, and Harris heard Mary say, 'He's just so quiet...' as he walked into the room.

'Harris, my dear,' she said, jumping up, 'why don't you sit here and have a good chat with Mr ... with Patrick.'

He sat. Patrick surveyed him for a few moments – longer than felt normal, with more precision than he had when they'd shaken hands in the hall. 'So, Harris ... er ... as I said, it's very sad about your parents. They were great people.'

Were they? Harris thought back to his parents, to the way they used to argue and bicker and moan at him, but also to the kind things they'd do, like take him to the cinema or ice-skating or a trip to Battersea Park or the aquarium. None of this added up to 'great' in his eyes, but more just what parents did. 'Great' sounded like they changed the world in some way, built extraordinary cities or found a cure for illnesses. They didn't do any of these things. But they did love him, he was certain of that.

'As I think Mrs Swallow may have explained to you, I knew your parents – my wife and I were family friends of theirs. I've even met you once or twice, when you were younger. I don't know if you remember?'

Harris hadn't recognised him at first, but now he properly looked at Patrick Moncrieff, he realised he had seen him before, although wouldn't have been able to place where. He noticed the man was quite good-looking, then wondered if that was a weird thing to notice in a man so much older than him. Without thinking what he was doing or stopping to wonder if the question was rude, he asked 'How old are you?'

Looking taken aback, Patrick answered 'I'm forty-one.'

Harris nodded, though he didn't know why. Patrick looked as though he could have been anything from thirty-two to forty-five. Any number within that range wouldn't have surprised him. His mother had been the same, managing to look both youthful and mature, ageless in a way some of his friends' mums, like Mary Swallow, never pulled off.

'I was wondering ... perhaps we could go for a walk in the park? I know it's a bit cold, but we could stop off at a café somewhere and get a hot drink. Would you like that?'

Harris wasn't sure he'd especially 'like' it, but he couldn't think of any real reason to say no. So they left the house and went for a walk in the nearby park, and he listened to Patrick talk about how he lived in a large house in Bath and had a son named Raphael who was a little bit older than Harris. Patrick said his wife, Isabelle, worked in the film industry and he asked if Harris liked movies. 'Yeah, don't mind them,' Harris replied with a shrug as he kicked a clump of fallen leaves off the pathway they were following. 'I prefer books, though. I like reading.' Patrick said that was great, that books were the foundation of a clever mind, and that he would buy Harris any books he wanted. They had a library that wasn't used much and Harris was welcome to take books from it. Harris's interest was awakened and his mind flashed instantly to the scene in the *Beauty and the Beast* where Belle is shown the enormous library by the beast and how this moment helped her fall in love with him. Would this be how he'd fall in love with the Moncrieff family, he wondered? Would they make him like them by giving him things? He'd never felt he'd gone without, but he'd also never felt 'wealthy' and as if money was no consideration. The thought of having whatever he wanted of a particular thing felt foreign to him, but not in a bad way.

'So, how about it, Harris?' Patrick said, 'Would you be up for trying out our family?'

Harris considered this for a few seconds, then said, 'I ... I think I'll be fine on my own. It's, like, kind of you and everything, but I'm old enough to be okay. I'll just live in my house. I'll go to school and everything. I won't bunk off and just do nothing.'

Patrick laughed – not an unkind laugh, but one that made Harris suddenly feel like a child who had said something very silly. 'I'm afraid you are too young for that. And besides, I don't know if you know this, but your parents' home was rented. They didn't own it. I helped them out a few times with money for the rent. And I'd like to carry on helping them out, now that you're alone in the world. Unless, of course, you'd prefer a children's home?'

Patrick must have known, he thought, that this wouldn't sound appealing to a fifteen-year-old boy. And although Harris felt he was being manoeuvred, he had to admit the thought of a large house with a well-stocked library sounded far more preferable than living with a bunch of other kids who had lost their parents. Or even with the Swallows, nice as they were.

But he couldn't escape the fact that the thing he'd really like to do would be to choose a third option: one that meant no change and that whisked him back in time to before his parents' deaths, to when everything was just fine, just ... normal. He knew it was foolish, that life didn't work like that outside of science fiction, but he wished it was possible just to undo moments in time, like using the backspace key for a Word document. Harris didn't say this, he didn't want Patrick to think he had gone mad in his grief. But he still hated the fact that not only was he having to negotiate his feelings of loss, he was also having to contemplate changes to his entire future. The ripple effect to every moment seemed huge, colossal, daunting. And that felt incredibly unfair. Unfair that he couldn't wait and think about this in years to come when he was in a better state to compute what was happening. Unfair that it even had to happen at all.

They had reached the café in the centre of the park and Patrick came to a stop outside it. 'Come, let's have a drink. I'll buy you a hot chocolate and a muffin. Then afterwards you can tell me what you've decided.'

Harris nodded and went inside. He appreciated Patrick wording it as if he had a choice in the matter, but he suspected he was actually being told what was happening rather than being asked to decide. Besides, if it had actually been a choice, he wasn't about to turn down it down. Some people – or orphans, for that is how he sometimes thought of himself – would kill for such a chance. A new life in a big country house with a family ready to welcome him in. All things considered, what could be better than that?

Chapter Six

PATRICK

Three-and-a-half years before the party

Patrick arrived back home in Bath at around eight o'clock after his trip to London to see Harris. He had missed dinner and found his wife sitting in the lounge by the fire working on her laptop. She said nothing when he came in. This wasn't a good sign.

'I saw the boy,' he said, sitting down, a brandy in his hand. 'It's a pity you couldn't join us.'

She didn't raise her eyes. 'I had work to do,' she said, flicking her hand at the laptop screen briefly, before continuing to type.

Patrick leaned forwards, trying to seek out her gaze. 'It will be all right. Harris, I mean. We've got a lot of space here, and he seems like a polite, quiet boy. I don't think he'll be any trouble. And I believe—' He stopped, thinking how to word the next bit. 'I mean ... he'll end up in a children's home, or whatever they call them these days, if we don't do this. As I said before. I think we owe it to Erin and John.'

Her eyes come up to meet his. The typing stopped. 'Do we?' Although it was a question, she said it more as a statement. The words, although said quietly, felt razor sharp. The silence was much worse than the typing. Patrick got up and went to stand over by the fire. He looked at the one photo on the mantlepiece in a silver frame. He and Isabelle and Raphael, smiling. Was it bad he couldn't remember where the picture had been taken? He couldn't even be precise about his son's age in the photo. He turned to look over at Isabelle, wondering if he should ask her, that it would offer something normal to talk about. But he decided against it. It worried it would draw attention to how their family unit might soon change.

'I...' he started to say, considered, then went on, 'I think he'll fit in well.'

She was still staring at him, her eyes trained like lasers. 'Will he?'

This second, short, loaded question, irritated Patrick. He didn't like the subtext. He thought people should either say what they meant or disguise it as best they could. This hidden-meaning thing that his wife was a master of frequently put his teeth on edge.

'Yes,' Patrick replied, nodding, 'I believe so.' He

smiled, trying to make it seem like they were having a pleasant – if important – discussion about the subject rather than this awkward experience he had to endure.

He knew why Isabelle was being like this. He knew what she was thinking. And he knew why she'd never say it out loud. Why they could never properly have this conversation in the way they really should.

Because that would mean facing up to things. That would mean showing cracks. And Isabelle didn't do cracks. She was made of iron, he knew it. She saw what she wanted, went for it, and always saw things through. She wasn't going to let whatever was happening here break her. This was a difficult situation to be in, but at least there was one advantage to it: he suspected his wife would rather let the boy come to live with them than risk the whole thing unravelling. In spite of this, though, he couldn't help making sure. And to do this, he felt the need to remind her of a few things.

'Of course, with your company doing so well, and so many film companies signing up for your services, I imagine you'll be quite busy over the coming months, anyway, won't you?'

He saw something tighten in Isabelle's face. 'What's that got to do with anything?'

He saw that this had riled her and was certain she knew what he was getting at. If she wanted to play the subtext game, she had to learn to be on the receiving end of it, he thought to himself, disliking the flash of resentment and anger that had flooded through him. He gripped the side of the mantlepiece and tried to keep his tone calm.

'I'm just saying, you probably won't have to deal with the boy much, with all the work you'll be doing. That's presuming the company carries on being as successful. I mean, the lease on those office premises in London – things can get expensive. The City of Westminster is a precarious place to set up business. A lot of renovations, a lot of costs, a lot of competing opportunities. I'm just saying I'll have to keep things under consideration, going forward. Make sure *my* very generous investment is … well, still worth it.'

Isabelle slammed her laptop closed. She'd gone completely white and Patrick could now see the pure fury in her eyes. 'How dare you threaten me, Patrick? How fucking dare you?' Her voice wasn't much more than a whisper, yet he could almost feel the walls reverberating as if she'd screamed at him.

'I'm not threatening anyone. I'm just saying that life is a balance. A continual weighing things up. Deciding what's important.'

She looked, for a moment, as if she actually would scream at him. But then she lowered her gaze to the floor. Stayed very still. That's when he knew he'd won. That when it came to it, they were on the same page. Harris would come to live at Bowen Hall. How smooth a transition it was going to be for all of them just remained to be seen.

'Will you meet him first?' Patrick asked her.

Her eyes returned to him for a few seconds more, then she said 'I doubt we'd be allowed to adopt a child without him meeting us both beforehand. Could you imagine social services or lawyers or anyone in authority allowing such a thing to happen? So I suppose I'll have to.'

Patrick stepped forward. Laid a hand on her shoulder. 'Thank you,' he said. He meant it, too. But if Isabelle had detected any genuine feeling in the words, she didn't let on. She didn't respond or even move. He took his hand away and she opened up the laptop and started to type again, words apparently flowing from her fingertips at once, as if she were a machine that simply had to be switched on.

He wasn't sure how long passed, but eventually the typing stopped again. Then Isabelle said, 'You're asking a lot of me, Patrick.'

Patrick held a breath, then let it out slowly, feeling his pulse quicken, trying to slow it. 'I know.'

'And I really don't appreciate the threats. I'm not someone for you to bribe, blackmail or manoeuvre.'

He felt himself starting to blush, a touch of shame now spreading through him. 'I'm sorry,' he said, quietly.

Silence followed this once again. He stayed where he

was for a minute or two, not wishing to be the first one to go up to bed, only to lie there wondering if Isabelle would be joining him. He decided to take matters into his own hands. 'I think I'll sleep in the Ebony room tonight.' This was the name they gave to the bedroom directly adjacent to theirs, where Patrick would often sleep if he'd got back from a work trip late and didn't want to disturb his wife.

'Do as you like,' she said with a sigh – a sound that could have suggested boredom if he hadn't known her better. 'You usually do.'

For a moment, amidst the unease, he felt the shame give way to anger. A sudden drive to defend himself, to tell her he was trying to do the right thing in a complex situation. But he didn't think he had the energy. Not now. So he went to bed, unaware of how things would pan out. Unaware what change he was bringing upon his family.

Chapter Seven

HARRIS

Three years and five months before the party

When Patrick arrived a week later to take Harris to his family home, he came alone rather than with his wife. Harris wondered why his wife Isabelle hadn't come, too. He had met her during a meeting with one of the more smiley child-services officials and the lawyer, Mr Booth. After the latter two had departed, Patrick and Isabelle had stayed for a strange, rather awkward dinner with the Swallows, with Mary heaping their plates with a lasagne she'd picked up from the local supermarket on her way home from work. Isabelle, who reminded Harris of the White Witch from *The Chronicles of Narnia*, looked at her plate as if Mary had just vomited on it, then proceeded to eat the mound of pasta and mince in incremental pieces lifted carefully from fork to mouth. Although her facial expressions may have told another story, she was generally polite to Mary and Mike and asked Harris the usual questions, such as, 'What are you studying at school?' and 'Do you have any favourite subjects?' and 'What hobbies do you have?' Although he recognised she was trying to make the most of a situation she seemed to be finding awkward, he didn't feel any motherly vibes coming off her. She was the complete opposite to Mary, who had instantly acted like a second mum to Harris the moment he'd arrived. He couldn't imagine Isabelle unwrapping a supermarket-purchased duvet and pulling on a Star Wars themed bed cover over it, or giving him a comforting warm hug when he thought about his parents and tears started to run down his face during an embarrassingly public moment. Isabelle was a different type of person. He wondered if she'd ever hugged anyone in her life. But he reminded himself that she and Patrick had a son, so they must be used to being parents and doing parent things. Perhaps they were just different parents to his own.

Alone with Patrick in the car, he was pleased the chat was kept to a minimum. Patrick occasionally asked him his thoughts on things, usually triggered by what was being discussed on Radio 4, which was playing in the background at a low volume.

Before too long, they had arrived at the Moncrieff's home, Bowen Hall. Patrick drove the car up the long driveway and slowed the car down to a crawl. Harris was confused by this for a moment, then realised Patrick must be doing it to heighten the impact of the house coming into view while he started to reel off facts about the property. 'The hall was modelled on West Wycombe Park, which itself was inspired by late-renaissance villas in Italy. Bowen was built in the twenties and they went for a much more quietly refined, white-coloured theme – it looks splendid, doesn't it?' After a short pause, once he'd realised he'd been asked a question, Harris nodded and assured him it was very impressive. It was true, it was impressive, but having grown up his entire life in a townhouse in the heart of a busy capital city, he didn't understand why a family of three would need so much space or what they would find to do with nothing around them but trees, fields and more trees.

'There's an annex, too; we tend to use it when we host parties, when more people than we can fit in the house want to stay over. And there's an outdoor swimming pool, but that remains covered during the winter, of course. When the weather warms up, you're welcome to use it.'

Patrick parked outside the front of the house, his car in a slanted position on the gravel. Harris wondered if his way of parking the car was a statement of sorts – *This is my kingdom, I'll park how I like* – rather than tucking his car tidily alongside the wall. Harris wasn't sure he liked this.

Inside, he found Isabelle in the cavernous opening

hallway. She'd just opened a letter from a pile of post on a small white table and set it down as they came in. 'Pleased you're both here, safe,' she said, with hardly any emotion in her voice. She didn't smile or embrace Harris but told him to leave all the bags near the door and their housekeeper, Emmeline, would take them upstairs.

'Do you like the Christmas tree?' Patrick asked, catching Harris looking at it. Harris nodded. It was a tall Norwegian spruce, decorated in gold and pearly-white baubles, which seemed to echo the whole colour scheme of the house – or at least the part he could see of it. 'There's one in practically every room,' Patrick said. 'We seem to have more each year.'

'That isn't true,' Isabelle said with a sigh, 'four trees each year. It doesn't vary. None in the bedrooms.'

'Although you could have one in your room, if you wish,' Patrick said to Harris, hurriedly. 'You could have a small one. I've seen them outside supermarkets.'

'Do what you like,' Isabelle said, with the tiniest of shrugs, 'but choose something nice – not some scratchy little thing you've found outside Asda.'

'I really don't need a tree in my room,' Harris said, feeling the whole thing was getting a bit out of hand.

'Let's get you settled upstairs,' Patrick said.

'I'll do that,' Isabelle cut in, 'I'm going up there anyway.'

Patrick nodded, although Harris saw him looking a bit uncertain.

'Come on,' Isabelle said impatiently. So Harris followed her, up the stairs, past another tall Christmas tree on the landing and down a row of doors. They got to the fifth one along and Isabelle opened it. 'Here we are. I'm sure it will be comfortable. Feel free to … I don't know … personalise it in some way.' She said all this with a lack of enthusiasm that Harris was fast learning was typical for her, although he nodded and said thank you in a way he hoped sounded grateful.

'I understand most of the contents of your old house are going into storage, but Patrick will take you to get some more of your things,' she said, walking further into the room. He could see why she said it – the whole place did look a bit bare. Clean, tidy and expensive, like a very nice cream-white toned hotel room, but without any character. It definitely wasn't the room of a teenage boy. It wasn't a room for anyone, really. A clatter on the landing announced the arrival of Patrick behind them with Harris's suitcases and bags.

'I said to leave those for Emmeline,' Isabelle said, sounding irritated.

'It's not fair to ask her to lug all this up the stairs,' Patrick said.

Isabelle murmured something about the housekeeper being paid actual money to do so, but Patrick ignored her.

'You've got a nice view of the garden from here,' he said striding over to the window.

Harris nodded and said, 'Thank you' again, because he couldn't think of anything else to say. It was both overwhelming and anti-climactic at the same time. He wasn't sure what he expected – perhaps some dark, creaking, cobweb-covered mansion from a storybook. But Bowen Hall looked more like a show home from one of his mother's magazines. He looked out of the window at the equally neat and expansive but unremarkable lawn and trees.

'Do you have any … questions?' Patrick asked.

Harris started to shake his head but then asked, 'Why is it called Bowen Hall?'

'It was the name of one of the previous owners. Long gone now. Aristocrats, I believe, but a lot of the house has been refurbished since then. To make it comfortable for us commoners.' He grinned. Harris nodded but didn't smile back.

'Let's go and meet Raphael,' Patrick said jovially. 'Come on.' He marched towards the door and out onto the landing. Isabelle didn't join them for this and instead walked back along the landing and down the stairs without saying anything.

'We'd best knock.' Patrick came to one of the doors and laughed, then seemed embarrassed about the laugh and cleared his throat awkwardly. 'Raphael,' he said, giving the door a sharp wrap with his knuckles. When there was no response, Patrick tutted and just opened the door.

The room was identical to the bedroom they'd just come from in terms of layout, but there had been a clear level of personalisation going on. The desk in the corner had books and pens and an iMac computer, the floor was scattered with clothes and magazines, and there were posters for movies – *Goodfellas* and *Die Hard* – on the wall. Lying astride the burgundy-coloured duvet, a laptop resting on his legs, was a teenage boy – clearly a year or two older than Harris. Even lying down, his long, athletic frame conveyed strength and power, the muscles on his arms visible through his shirt and the dark green Polo Ralph Lauren cardigan he was wearing. His eyes flicked over to the door as we entered.

'Raphael, get up and say hello,' Patrick ordered sternly.

The boy gave an almost theatrically long sigh, as if nothing could have bored him more, and then got to his feet. He strolled lazily over to Harris and held out his hand. Harris shook it, unsurprised that Raphael's large hand and strong grip nearly crushed his. It was immediately clear: Harris was not a welcome addition to the household for Raphael Moncrieff.

Although Isabelle didn't exactly seem overjoyed with Harris's arrival, at least her reaction hadn't been so full of contempt or as openly hostile. The expression her son was giving Harris now, left him in no doubt what Raphael felt about him.

'I'll leave you both to get acquainted,' Patrick said, then left the room.

Harris was silently mortified to be left alone with this large, unfriendly older boy. He looked up at him, desperate for something to say, but no words arrived. He felt completely inadequate in every way. His shapeless, baggy tracksuit felt repellently unsophisticated compared to this boy's casually preppy attire. The more he looked at Raphael's neatly cut and styled dark-blond hair, his height, his muscles and slim waist, the shorter and more overweight Harris felt. This boy had good looks, an enviable physique and undeniable presence. All the things Harris felt he could never match up to.

'Why are you staring at me?' Raphael said.

'I ... sorry, I...' Harris started to say, although his words seemed to fall on deaf ears. Raphael had walked back to the bed and flung himself down, scooping up the laptop from the edge of the mattress. He started to click away on it, his jaw clenched, his eyes focused on the screen and the screen only. And Harris just stood there, unsure what to do.

Eventually, after what felt like a lifetime, Raphael spoke. 'Oh do just fuck off,' he said.

Harris stood frozen to the spot for a few seconds more. Then he left the room.

Chapter Eight

HARRIS

The day of the party

Harris and Raphael go downstairs to 'help out' with the party preparations, although Harris doubts much helping will occur. Raphael's mood shows no signs of improving and he mooches about the kitchen, then the library, then the living room, occasionally picking up or moving something, like a plate or a vase, then setting it back down again, as if these small actions will give off the sense of being busy and involved.

A commotion outside ends up bringing them both to the French windows of the library. Isabelle and Emmeline are on the patio, the latter standing on the steps leading down to the lawn and the former towering above her, shouting. 'You've already come close to wrecking this party by your botched chair order – I don't understand why you find it so hard to follow some simple bloody instructions! Considering how much we've done for you.'

This seemed to be the last straw for Emmeline. Pulling off her apron and tossing it aside, she throws her hands in the air. 'I'm done, I'm fucking done with you all. There's only so much a normal fucking person can take. Just because your precious sodding boy has knocked up his bloody tutor at uni doesn't mean the whole world has to go into meltdown! Nobody really fucking cares, you know! I've stuck this job out for eight years – eight fucking awful years of being ordered about and treated like a servant—'

'Well, here's a bloody news flash for you, dear,' Isabelle says with ice in her voice, 'you are a fucking servant.'

The slap rings out like a shot. Emmeline looks horrified the second her hand comes away from Mrs Moncrieff's face. Harris and Raphael rush over to Isabelle.

'Mum, are you okay?' Raphael says, running round to face her. Before she can answer, he turns to Emmeline and says, 'What the hell is wrong with you?'

'I'm sorry...' Emmeline mutters, a tear falling down her face. She looks shaken and shocked by her own actions.

Isabelle, who has been rendered momentarily silent, seems to be quickly regaining the power of speech, one hand clasped to where Emmeline struck her. 'How *dare* you assault me. Yes, you *assaulted* me. An actual *crime*. You ungrateful girl.'

'Please … no… It was just a slap…'

'*Just* a slap?' Isabelle says, drawing herself up to her full height, which is a good inch or two taller than the weeping housekeeper. 'Well, that might be *just* a slap in whatever violent hovel you called home before we welcomed you into our house—'

'I'm from *Ealing*!'

'—but I can tell you, attacks like that are not tolerated here. Not at all.'

'Mum,' Raphael says uneasily, perhaps sensing that she is going too far, but Isabelle dodges away from his comforting hand on her shoulder and takes a step closer to Emmeline.

'You're fired,' she says, curtly. 'With immediate effect.'

'I think I already resigned,' says Emmeline, then takes a step back down the steps, clearly worried Isabelle might fly at her.

There is a moment's pause, then Isabelle says, 'I'm going to phone the police.'

'Oh, come on, Mum,' Raphael says as Isabelle stalks past him and into the house. 'Mum, please, this is pointless…'

'I'm *phoning!*' she shouts back.

Harris tries to offer what he hopes is a comforting look to Emmeline, but he doubts she notices as she too rushes past.

'Fuck this,' she says. 'Sorry to spoil your day, Raphael, I really am, but I'm not going to wait here to be arrested.'

'Woah, Emmeline, wait a sec,' Raphael says, walking after her as she disappears off around the side of the house. Harris follows. He isn't sure if this sort of drama is useful for his nerves today, but like Raphael he cares for Emmeline and finds seeing her so distressed upsetting in itself.

'Mum's not going to phone the police,' Raphael calls after her. 'Please don't leave, not ... not today.'

Emmeline comes to a stop, about four metres away from where Raphael stands. Harris watches, standing back from them as she walks over to Raphael and puts her hand on his shoulder, using the other to wipe a tear away.

'Oh, God, look at you. So handsome. You've spent too long, Raphael, trying to figure out what you want.'

Raphael starts to stutter in response, but Emmeline shakes her head. 'It's okay, just ... just do what's good for you, Raphael. And Harris,' she says, turning to look at him. 'Stop sitting on the sidelines and stand up to those self-indulgent people. Sorry to talk about your parents that way, Raphael, but they … they should have been better … to both of you.' Then she leaves, walking away from them to where her car is parked.

'Well … bloody hell…' Raphael says, puffing his cheeks out.

'Yeah, that was … unexpected,' says Harris. He hopes Isabelle's threat of the police really is an empty one. It really wouldn't do to have a police presence here, not today. No matter for how trivial a reason.

'Come on,' Raphael says, 'I need a smoke.'

They seek refuge in one of the greenhouses to the north of the house, Raphael puffing away on a large Cuban cigar, Harris trying not to grimace at the smell of the smoke cloud floating his way. They stand together without talking for a while. They have silences like this, he and Raphael, that sometimes feel almost companionable. Sometimes Harris catches himself feeling quite warmly towards him. Then he reminds himself of what Raphael has done. The things Harris has seen. What has gone on and, to an extent, continues to go on between them. And his warm feelings end and became bitter once more.

'Good stuff, this,' Raphael says, looking at the cigar in his hand. Harris has never seen him smoke a cigarette or take illegal drugs, but he knows of his fondness for cigars. A pretentious choice, Harris has always thought. He suspects Raphael likes the idea of appearing an 'upper-class gentleman', aspiring to one day being the wise man in the leather-backed chair at a men-only posh club in Westminster, giving nuggets of wisdom to the younger members.

'You make it sound as if you're smoking weed or crack,' Harris replies.

Raphael laughs. 'I'll miss Emmeline,' he says, letting out a deep breath of smoke. 'There was a time when I thought she fancied me, you know.'

Harris scoffs. 'She's like fifteen years older than you.'

Raphael tilts his head and smirks. 'I wouldn't have said no.'

'I would. Have said no, that is. She was definitely more of a maternal figure for me. When I first came here she was a lot more friendly than—'

'Me, I know, I know,' Raphael says, rolling his eyes.'

'I was going to say your mother,' Harris replies, with a half smile. 'But yeah, you were … interesting, when I arrived.' Harris watches Raphael's face closely, who keeps his eyes ahead, not meeting his. Then he decides to ask a question he has been wondering. And one he knows Raphael won't like. 'Does Lauren know?'

Raphael frowns. 'Does my fiancé know how I felt about our housekeeper?'

'No, of course not,' Harris says, leaning back against one of the potting benches. 'I meant – well, does she *know*?'

'What are you *on* about?'

Harris chooses his moment, looks him straight in the eyes, then says, 'About what happened between us?'

The colour goes out of Raphael's cheeks in an instant. He looks back at Harris, hard, his jaw jutting out defensively. 'I don't know what you're talking about, Harris.'

'That's a no, then,' Harris says, holding his gaze.

Raphael throws his cigar down onto the concrete floor and stamps on it viciously. He then comes very close up to Harris and says 'Why the fuck would you say that to me? What the fuck... Why would you say that to me *now*? *Today*? I thought ... I thought...'

'You thought what?' Harris asks, refusing to be intimidated, 'You thought we were best pals? *Really*?'

Raphael takes a step back, his eyes darting everywhere, like a fox in a trap, his breathing clearly quickening, perspiration now visible on his neck. 'If you say one word of this – if you say anything else like this today, or on any other day, I ... I...' He then leans in close to Harris again, holding his shoulder so hard that Harris sees dots of pain in his vision. 'I will fucking *kill you*.' These last words are almost a whisper, but it feels as though he's shouted them at close range. A myriad of thoughts rush through Harris's mind at that point. Things that have happened in the past. Things that will happen today. Secrets that nobody in the family will want to believe. Incidents that have been buried for years. Video footage that will change everyone's view of Raphael forever.

It looks as though Raphael is going to say something else. A pause, where the two of them look at each other, eyes locked. Then Raphael drops his gaze and leaves the greenhouse, leaving Harris alone, shaking a little. But smiling.

Chapter Nine

HARRIS

Three years before the party

As time passed, with weeks turning into months, Harris started to feel more settled at Bowen Hall, if not exactly at home. During his time at the Swallow's house, he'd felt very much in limbo, knowing it was only temporary. He liked the fact he had now reached a 'final stop'. A new normal. Or as normal as he was going to get for the moment.

He made efforts to personalise his room, bringing some of his belongings back from the storage unit containing things from his old house. Having a wider range of clothes, books and various items (like a lava lamp he'd got for his fourteenth birthday, a trophy from a literature quiz tournament at school, and a zip-up set of artist's pastels) made him feel a connection to the past, but they felt out of place in the sleek, catalogue-ready tidiness of the Moncrieff's home.

Isabelle and Patrick mostly kept out of his way. Isabelle, it seemed, by choice, since she was home most of the time, working from her downstairs office, and Patrick due to travelling for his job. When he was home, he would apologise for constantly having to be away for work, to which Harris just shrugged and replied, 'Yeah, sure, no worries', generally because he didn't know what else to say. Emmeline, the very smiley and rather attractive housekeeper was more of a parent to him in those first few weeks than anyone else in the house. He initially found it embarrassing when she knocked on his bedroom door and said she was 'just popping in to collect the washing' and then proceed to gather up handfuls of his clothes from the laundry bin in the corner of the room. Or when she'd stick her head round the door and offer him a sandwich or toast or a Coke, or perhaps a hot drink. But the more she did these caring tasks, always with a welcoming smile, the happier and more settled he felt at Bowen Hall. She even, on occasion, would catch him looking wistfully out the window or walking slowly up the stairs and she'd put a hand on his shoulder and ask him if he was okay. He always nodded hurriedly and shuffled away to his room, but he appreciated the kind gesture.

Raphael, on the other hand, never said anything kind or well-meaning during those early weeks. He either took his mother's lead by pretending Harris barely existed, or he would make pointed and unkind comments or noises, like a scoffing sound when he saw Harris getting himself breakfast in the mornings, as if the boy's very presence was a preposterous joke. He'd shake his head and sneer when they bumped into each other on the landing, or roll his eyes if Harris made a comment about something – anything, no matter how mild – during dinner.

As the weeks went on, he started to suspect Raphael was playing tricks on him; childish games of the kind he'd have thought childish for a boy of Raphael's age. They'd usually be minor things, involving items disappearing, that could easily be explained away. Some nights he'd come back from brushing his teeth and his pillowcases would have vanished from his bed. Other nights he'd get out the bath and find there to be no towels in the wicker hamper that usually housed them in abundance. Or he'd open one of his drawers and find all his socks had disappeared, or the right foot of his trainers had gone walkabout, or the clock on his bedroom wall would be upside down. These things usually worked themselves out – items would turn up, usually a day or two later, and the same trick was never repeated twice. Harris would lie awake at night, thinking about all this – and each time it happened, it sent him into another spiral of confusion, hurt and anger. He decided not to tell Isabelle or Patrick about these occurrences, nor did he confront Raphael. He had no proof, nor did he want to cause a row or sound like he was telling tales. But he knew it was Raphael. After each of these instances, he'd always have a smug look about him – even more than usual – and Harris would be in no doubt. Raphael hated him. Hated him being in his home, sharing his time with him at meals, being part of the family's preparations for Christmas. But Harris kept hold of the advice his mother had given him when he'd had a scuffle in the playground aged eleven: *always ignore bullies, it's amazing how quickly they tire of their own silly games.*

Eventually, Raphael did tire. The week of Christmas came and Harris noticed a reduction in the frequency of the vanishings. On Christmas Eve, Harris woke to find it had snowed in the night and the view from his bedroom window looked like a scene from a Christmas card. He'd got up to go and tell his mum to come and see it. It had been a while since he'd made such an error, a fleeting moment when he forgot that she and his dad were gone, but it crushed him each time it occurred, even more so on this day, which in years before was always a happy one involving visitors dropping by with presents and mince pies by the fire.

There were indeed mince pies and a fire at the Moncrieff's though it all felt very different. The fire was real but modern, sporting a glass and cream panel design that felt the opposite of cosy. The mince pies weren't homemade, but expensive and from a shop and unpacked onto a white plate where they all looked neat and perfect in a very impersonal way.

That evening, the Moncrieffs held a gathering involving two other families they knew, the Nightlys and the Sutherlands. Harris had no idea what the Nightlys did, but he'd overheard that the Sutherlands were one part hedge-fund manager (the male, Antonio) and one part best-selling author (the female, Sarah). They mingled around, chatting and eating nibbles, with a light jazz-piano-style arrangement of Christmas carols playing from an invisible sound system. The Sutherlands brought with them a son Raphael's age, whom he seemed to know well, though Harris gleaned from eavesdropping on their conversation that they went to different schools. Both Isabelle and Patrick had mentioned to Harris that he could exit the evening at any point and go to his room if he wished. Patrick said this with apparent kindness and understanding whilst Isabelle's wording and tone made Harris suspect she'd just like him out of the way.

To an extent, the guests seemed polite and interested in Harris, with the Sutherlands passing on their condolences. If the subject got too near his parents, he noticed Isabelle swiftly moved it on. He listened a bit to their discussions, sitting by the fire and starting to feel more morose as the evening went on. The women had settled themselves not far from Harris, apparently having a conversation about Sarah Sutherland's disenchantment with her current publisher and the way they packaged her 'equestrian romance' books.

'Oh, the whole literary landscape has been so strange and unpredictable since the pandemic,' she said, as the other woman, Anita Nightly, nodded sympathetically. 'It's hard to keep track of what the '*in* thing' is. Maybe I should just chuck it all in and write a sodding mindfulness book or something.'

Anita frowned, popping the end of a mince pie crust into her mouth. 'Mindfulness is *so* 2015, darling,' she said. 'No, it's now all about being the perfect mother. Or fitness and diet books about how it's now fine to eat doughnuts again. You could write one of those.'

Sarah laughs. 'Not exactly my area. No, I'll stay with my horse novels. I enjoy writing them, at least. I just wish my publisher would include them in more literary-prize submissions. But apparently I'm not 'literary' enough.' She raised a free hand and made some vague air quotes. 'But I have no idea how to make a book more *literary*.'

'Oh, my dear, that's easy,' said Anita, 'just delete all the speech marks and embrace obfuscation.'

'I'm not sure you're being particularly helpful,' said Sarah, half laughing.

'Failing that, ditch all sense of sentence structure and paragraph breaks altogether. You'll be at that Booker dinner in no time.'

'That isn't really how it works, Anita,' said Sarah.

'You should ask Isabelle if one of her Hollywood contacts could make a film of your books.'

'Again, that's not really how it all—'

'I'm sure she's got her ways and means,' Anita continued, turning her neck to see Isabelle talking to Patrick and the two other husbands. 'She has a ruthless side you know.' Anita paused, her mouth going very thin for a moment, still looking over at Isabelle. 'Ruthless,' she said again. 'Some people say she'd do *anything* to get what she wants.'

'Well, I doubt my books are on her radar,' said Sarah with a chuckle.

Anita rolled her eyes and went to take another sip of mulled wine. As she did so, her gaze rested on Harris. A few minutes later she detached herself from the discussion with Sarah and came over to him. 'Can I sit with you?' she asked, then sat in the chair opposite him without waiting for an answer. 'I still can't get to grips with who you actually *are*.' It wasn't exactly a question, but she raised her eyebrows as she sipped at her wine, staring at Harris as though she expected an explanation.

'I'm ... living here now,' he replied, blandly.

'Yes, yes, I know that,' Anita said, batting in the air, keeping her achingly posh voice low, 'I just wondered about your family connection to the Moncrieffs. They've never mentioned you. And I've never heard of your family. Odd, wouldn't you think?'

Harris shrugged.

'You sound very … London,' she said, and didn't make it sound like a compliment.

'I lived in London, yes.'

'Whereabouts?'

Harris cast an eye about, wondering if either Patrick or Isabelle might come to his rescue, but the former had his back to him and the latter had gone to the kitchen.

'Er … Westminster.'

'Now this *is* very odd,' Anita said, crossing her legs and leaning forward, 'because my husband and I live in Westminster. Don't you think we would have met, if our families mixed in the same circles?'

When Harris didn't answer, she leaned back and narrowed her eyes. 'Which school?'

'Pardon?'

'Which school did you attend?'

'Westminster City School.'

She made a face as though she'd eaten something sour. 'I think there's a story here,' she said, slowly, 'a story I don't know, and I do like to be in the know, so to speak.' She looked over at Patrick, then back at Harris. 'Interesting,' she said, 'very interesting.' She took another sip of wine, then got up and walked away.

Chapter Ten

HARRIS

Three years before the party

Shortly after his interrogation from Anita Nightly, Harris noticed Isabelle had returned to the room, so he ventured to the kitchen. The fire had made him feel uncomfortably hot, especially in the old hoodie he'd grabbed from his cupboard (he'd seen Isabelle looking at it as if she'd like nothing better than to fling it in a bag destined for a charity shop).

In the kitchen, he filled one of the large tumblers with filtered water from the fridge dispenser and turned to leave, only to find himself confronted with both Raphael and the Sutherland boy.

'Move,' Raphael said to him.

'We've been tasked to find more mince pies,' the other boy said, sounding much friendlier in comparison.

Harris nodded at the plate of them on the side and the boy smiled and picked it up. Raphael's surly expression, however, remained resolute.

'Been eating them out here in secret, have you?' he sneered.

'What?' Harris replied, genuinely puzzled.

'Well, look at the size of you. You've clearly been eating too much of something.' He laughed and looked at his friend, clearly expecting him to laugh, too. But he didn't get the result he was looking for and a tense silence fell across the room.

'Why are you so fucking horrible?' Harris said, surprising himself. It was the first time he'd properly spoken back to Raphael and he waited nervously to see what result his words would have. Raphael looked taken aback at first, but recovered quickly, parroting back Harris's words and mimicking his accent. The Sutherland boy shifted, looking embarrassed. It was clear Raphael's approach wasn't working to his advantage, making him seem childish and cruel.

Harris just looked at him and Raphael looked back, his face going red. Then Harris set down the glass on the kitchen island, walked round the two boys in front of him and left the room.

Inside his bedroom, Harris sat on his bed, too cross to cry, too sad to think about Christmas. He didn't know what he felt, didn't know how to take Raphael's bullying or whether to tell Patrick or Isabelle about it. As time ticked on, he got up and went to the mirror. He took off his top and stood facing his reflection, touching his torso. He wasn't morbidly obese, he knew that, but he also knew he could take hold of more flesh in his hands around his middle than he would like. He'd never really been teased due to his weight before now, even if he'd always been fairly rubbish at sport in school. 'Fuck him,' he said out loud, defiantly, and in the silence he could almost hear Raphael echoing his words back in an exaggerated accent, mocking the perceived class difference between them.

That night, Harris came up with a plan. As the guests departed downstairs and the house fell silent, he sat at the desk in his room on his laptop. In a blank Word document he put together a diary for the weeks ahead, finding exercise regimes and home workouts, diet plans and healthy-eating tips. He found YouTube links, articles, expert hacks and instructions from famous influencers. He put it all down, breaking everything up into manageable days, with columns on each page where he could measure his progress. 'I'll fucking show him,' he muttered under his breath as he saved the doc and went to bed. By the time his head hit the pillow, all thoughts of

Christmas and the sadness he'd felt hours before had disappeared.

Over the festive period, Harris worked hard on his exercises, spending most of the time in his room, or going out for very early morning runs or brisk walks around the grounds in the freezing December air, trudging through snow, ice and then, as January arrived, rain. For meals, he continued to eat whatever was given to him – the food prepared by Isabelle or the kindly housekeeper Emmeline was never particularly unhealthy – but banned himself from going back for seconds or snacking in between.

In the evenings, he spent an hour or so each day watching videos online about refining one's accent and pronunciation. Whilst he didn't want the change in his voice to be radical enough to make people think he was putting it on or sounding overly affected, he was determined to dilute the current London slant to his vowels, and at the very least sound less noticeable. Less separate. Less of an outsider.

When his school uniform arrived shortly before the start of term at his new school, Harris was encouraged to find it already felt too large for him. Even after just two weeks, his work was paying off.

His start at school wasn't as bad as he'd expected,

and although he found himself mixing with boys from very different backgrounds, he found most people friendly and even started to make friends.

On a weekend when Patrick was in the US and Isabelle was in London with Raphael, Harris got a taxi to the nearby town and paid for a haircut – a much shorter, tidier cut than he'd ever had before. Afterwards he went to John Lewis and bought clothes in a similar style to the ones he'd seen the Moncrieffs wear – the Oxford shirts, the dark blue jeans and beige trousers, cardigans, jumpers. Patrick had been putting a generous amount of 'spending money' into his account every month and he'd barely touched any of it, but the balance was considerably lighter when he walked out of the store with bulging carrier bags and an entirely new wardrobe.

Back in his room, he tried on his new clothes and was startled at how different he looked. The cumulative effect of his weight loss, haircut and new attire added up to a considerable transformation and he wondered if he'd been silly not to document it somehow with those 'before and after' shots people shared on Instagram. He'd occasionally liked looking at those, and they had served as motivation prompts when the process got tough, but he'd always suspected those guys were a bit too 'poser-y' for his liking. He liked the idea of his project almost functioning by stealth, allowing the sudden change to creep up on people, when they'd glance at him and wonder how they could have ever overlooked him before.

Harris turned sixteen, and although he said he didn't want to do anything and certainly no fuss, Patrick still organised a bespoke cake to be sent to the house with his name iced on it. He had a generously sized slice to be polite, then resisted any further offers. He was still keeping his food intake carefully controlled and now knew, for the first time in his life, how much energy was contained in a single slice of cake and how easy it was to enjoy high-sugar treats whilst still maintaining a healthy lifestyle. In some ways, he liked thinking this way about food, removing the emotion and sense of comfort from it and instead considering it as a stark science with all the psychological layers stripped back.

As January became February, he started to get more attention – Isabelle and Patrick commented on how smart he was looking and even teachers seemed to be nicer and more attentive.

And someone else had started to notice him, too. On the first night of the half-term break, Harris had come home, finished a workout and taken a shower. Back in his room, he dropped his towel onto the floor and pulled on some pyjama trousers. Glancing in his mirror, he saw movement. Raphael had been hovering by his bedroom door, looking at him in a way he never had before.

Chapter Eleven

LAUREN

The day of the party

L auren has been coaching her parents the whole way to the party, reminding them of people's names, of what to say and what not to say and how to not let slip about the pregnancy.

'Hardly likely to do that,' her father says with a hollow laugh. 'Your mother would bloody kill me.'

'Thank goodness you're not showing yet, it just looks like you've gained a bit of weight,' her mother murmurs, apparently unbothered by how her daughter might take this.

Lauren does her best to keep smiling throughout it all. She always maintains a positive attitude, whatever life throws at her. It's always been her mentality that what you put into life, you get out of it. She was a great believer in karma, 'manifesting' and giving out positive energy. To help her journey through life and aid the mood of everyone around her, she frequently posts inspirational quotes and affirmations on her social media accounts and follows many others that do the same. So she reminds herself to count all the things she is grateful for when her father's car turns into the driveway of the Moncrieff's home (gratitude is an essential part of her positivity practice). She is grateful for … for… Her mind goes into its usual spasm of panic, in case she can't think of something, but the weather is always at hand – the sunshine and warm temperatures on this glorious spring day.

'It's a beautiful day,' Lauren says out loud (another thing she always tries to do, to really claim her thoughts and make them more tangible). 'We've been so lucky with the weather.'

'It's too hot,' grumbles her father.

'I wouldn't be surprised if it rained,' says her mother.

Lauren turns her thoughts to her boyfriend – no, *fiancé* – the man who will, in a month's time, meet her at the end of the aisle and say 'I do'.

'I'm looking forward to seeing Raphy all smart. I wonder what he's up to now,' she wonders aloud, valiantly keeping her tone light and airy.

'Probably doing his homework,' her father says with another of his empty laughs. The age difference between her and Raphael, with him being seven years younger, has become a regular source of digs from her parents. They frequently make it clear how strange and inappropriate they find the situation. Only once has she pointed out that her age difference to her fiancé is only one year more than the age difference between the two of them, though she is well aware that since her dad is the senior in the marriage, society has less interest in the difference than if it had been her mother who was the elder.

They drive slowly up to the house. 'It's beautiful, isn't it?' Lauren says, misinterpreting her mother's sigh for a gasp of wonder.

'We just need to get this done. Once you're married all will be fine,' she says to Lauren as her father parks the car.

'Everything's fine now, already. We don't need to get anything over with. Everything's splendid.' Lauren says all this whilst beaming. Her mother does not return the smile.

'No, my dear, it's not, but let's not go over that again,' she says, shooting a purposeful look at her daughter's stomach area.

'Lauren, darling,' calls Isabelle as she walks down from the house, 'so lovely to see you again.'

'Hi Isabelle!' Lauren says, beaming as she walks across the gravel to embrace her future mother-in-law. 'You remember my parents?'

'Of course,' replies Isabelle and steps forward to greet them. 'It's, um, lovely to see you again.'

Their first meeting had been at a restaurant in Oxford where the plan for a shortened engagement and hasty wedding had been hatched. Although she had done her utmost to positively reframe this difficult meeting in her mind, Lauren couldn't help but feel Isabelle's 'um' to be an oblique reference to the awkwardness of that occasion.

Lauren's smile froze for a moment as she looked closer at Isabelle's face. 'Your cheek looks rather red – is everything okay?'

Isabelle raised a hand to her face. 'Oh, yes, I … I had an altercation. With the mad housekeeper. She's gone now.'

Lauren didn't hide her shock, 'Oh, gosh,' she said, 'Emmeline? She attacked you?'

Isabelle looked awkwardly over her shoulder at Lauren's parents and winced. Lauren could tell she would prefer not to go into it all at this moment, but she was too curious to bail her out of it. 'We just had a disagreement about the chairs… Well, it doesn't matter now. I threatened to call the police and that seemed to get rid of her.'

'But … hasn't she been with your family for a very long time? Years?'

Isabelle gives a brisk nod that clearly indicates the discussion about the fired housekeeper is over. 'So …

shall we...' Isabelle leads them through the house, inviting them to leave their bags and coats inside, then takes them out to the garden, where the party will be held. Raphael is nowhere to be seen and after asking Isabelle twice and then Patrick once, when he had joined them to say hello, Lauren doesn't feel she can ask a fourth time where her fiancé has got to. She can't help but feel hurt and annoyed that he wasn't waiting on the driveway to welcome them, and that he decided to spend the night before at his family home rather than wake up with his fiancé on the day of their engagement party. Indeed, his enthusiasm for the whole subject of the wedding has seemed limited at best, non-existent at worst. She reassures herself frequently that a lesser bride-to-be would allow this to cloud her mind with doubts and concerns, but she is stronger than most other brides-to-be and decides to put down Raphy's reluctance to typical male disinterest about 'wedding stuff' and a dislike of fuss.

Raphael is eventually located smoking near the greenhouses. He appears particularly troubled about something and Lauren is disappointed to see that her presence doesn't do much to lift him out of his mood. 'Raphy, my parents are here. They've come to celebrate our union, along with a lot of guests,' she says, tentatively, 'so perhaps we should put out the cigarette and smile and come round to greet the people who have travelled far and wide to celebrate this special day with us.' She then spots Harris walking back round the side of the house, looking as though he's going to sneak inside. She stops him with a wave, walking over to the boy and says how thrilled she is that he's here.

'Wouldn't miss it for the world,' says Harris grinning. For a moment she feels she can see something else in his face she isn't quite sure about, a knowing smile, as though he's amused about something. But they're interrupted by Raphael, who says they should go round to the front of the house to greet more guests.

Slightly annoyed that he has now taken it upon himself to prompt her to be sociable, when moments before their roles were reversed, she puts on her well-practised, living-her-best-life smile and says, 'I'm sure I'll see you later,' to Harris.

Over the course of the next half hour she beams, embraces, kisses cheeks, laughs and does everything she hopes a glowing, delighted fiancée should do. We really have been blessed with the weather, she thinks to herself. Everyone is being very friendly, and, if she is correct in her assumption, nobody has spotted any sign of the pregnancy about her or the fact that she is drinking Nozeco instead of champagne. However, during a trip inside to use the loo she feels her happy demeanour falter when she overhears two male voices. Inside one of the rooms off the hallway, she can hear Patrick and Harris talking. The elder man says, 'I'm sorry for what we said to each other. I think you have the wrong idea about ... well, about a lot of things. I know I should have spoken to you sooner. Tried to make up for everything. I think I rather spoilt Christmas, and then when you went back to London early, I was ... well, I was disappointed in myself.'

Intrigued, but feeling it would be wrong to eavesdrop, Lauren hovers in the hallway, gripped by indecision. She fancies her nose needs dabbing so she allows herself a considerable amount of time to very quietly take a tissue from the carved, wooden box on a small table to her left, fold it in her hand and raises it to her face. With this activity now the primary reason for her being in the hallway (or so she tells herself) it isn't her fault if she overhears a conversation within the vicinity.

'I just wanted you to know,' Patrick says, 'that the house wasn't, like, a bribe or anything. But I thank you for not talking to Isabelle or Raphael about it. Basically, the house is yours. If you want it.'

Silence follows for a few seconds. Lauren leans towards the doorway where the voices have been coming from. Then she hears Harris. 'I'll think about it. In any case, I don't want to spoil today.' There's a pause, and then he adds, 'This is a day to be remembered, I'm sure you'll agree.' Then the door opens and Harris walks out. She hurries to move, as if she's only just turned into the hallway herself, but it doesn't seem necessary – Harris barely seems to notice her.

Lauren walks away before her future father-in-law comes out of the room and finds her there. Although she knows that whatever row Patrick and Harris has had isn't really any of her business, she can't help but feel troubled from the exchange she's overheard. This family has secrets, she thinks, as she locates a downstairs bathroom and shuts herself inside. And secrets have the power to destabilise even the most stable of families.

Chapter Twelve

RAPHAEL

Three years before the party

Raphael Moncrieff liked women. This is what he told himself whenever he felt he needed reminding of the fact. And he wasn't lying to himself – at least, he didn't think he was. He *did* like women – he would notice when an attractive girl walked by and felt desire when he saw them in films. He occasionally watched porn, focused on women. Well, there'd be some guys involved, but the videos were all clearly shot with the focus on the woman's naked form.

But that was only half of the story. Perhaps not even half. Maybe thirty per cent of the story. Or a strong twenty per cent. The other seventy or eighty per cent of the story consisted of chapters he hadn't read. Chapters of his mind. He hadn't even properly acknowledged those chapters were there. It was easier to think of them as blank pages – pages he occasionally snuck a look at. If he went through life with his full story only partly read, he figured he could live with that.

He didn't feel any animosity towards guys who did explore that part of themselves. He had friends at school who were openly gay and didn't seem to find it much of a talking point. There were some other guys at school who practically celebrated it as though it were the only aspect of their lives worth talking about, and he found that a bit irritating. But overall, he was jealous of the guys, heterosexual or gay, who knew that they were one hundred per cent into one half of the human race, and very much *not* into the other half. He kept telling himself he was strange, that he should have things figured out, how he was like a clichéd repression case, like characters you'd find in TV dramas or soaps from decades ago who would have a tortured 'coming out' storyline after years of bottling everything up. In this day and age, it was all supposed to be no big deal. Or a major big deal, but a good big deal. He couldn't keep up with what the media, society, Instagram and his friends were saying these days. Whatever it was, they all seemed so *sure*. About everything. Things weren't as clear-cut for Raphael. And he really wished they were.

So Raphael Moncrieff had buried an àspect of himself so that it was out of sight and impossible to detect. And he thought he was doing a really good job of it. He'd lost his virginity to a girl when he was sixteen (a cousin of his best friend, Theo, who was visiting for their joint-sixteenth-birthday party), and became known at school as a 'player' with the girls in the sixth form, making sure he was seen kissing or going off to bed with at least one of them at any party, prom or celebration he attended. He didn't necessarily mind doing all this as such – he enjoyed a lot of it – but it still required effort. It required stamina. A stamina that started to be tested when Harris joined the family.

At first, Raphael hadn't looked twice at Harris, and if he did, it was to sneer at his awful tracksuits that looked like he'd just been released from prison, or to roll his eyes at something idiotic he'd said in that awful common accent that put his teeth on edge. But then things started to change. Harris started to change. Like a landscape changing from winter into spring, this dull, unremarkable boy had started to – well, there was no other word for it – blossom before his very eyes. He didn't know what the boy was doing or why he was doing it, but the change was so rapid and notable, he was certain it must be deliberate.

One night, he was crossing the landing when he saw Harris going into his bedroom, shirtless, with a towel wrapped around him. He'd had his hair cut closer to Raphael's own short blonde style. And he hadn't just lost weight; he'd gained muscle mass too, the definition in his abs and arms was much more prominent.

Why was he doing this? Raphael thought to himself as he edged closer to the boy's open doorway, his heart leaping as he saw him drop his towel and stand in the room, naked, beautiful even.

Beautiful. Had he really just used such a word to describe a boy – a boy he found annoying, irritating, confusing. A boy he didn't want living here in the first place. Some preposterous charity case he was sure his parents were taking on just to look good. Pretend they cared.

Then another thought crossed his mind. *Did he know something? Suspect something? Was he doing this to deliberately mess with him?* He watched as Harris pulled on some pyjama bottoms and turned to look in the mirror. That was when their eyes met.

Raphael froze for a few seconds, both of them staring at each other. Then he fled, marching down the landing to his room and heading inside, closing the door. He collapsed onto his bed, screwing up a pillow into his face, all the while saying 'Fuck, fuck, fuck, fuck,' to himself. He felt his heart pounding, blood rushing to his head. He felt sick. But a small part of him felt something else. Excitement. A lurching, thrilling feeling, as if he were on a roller coaster that was teetering on the verge of the sharpest of dips.

There were going to be very difficult times ahead for him. He could feel it.

Chapter Thirteen

HARRIS

Three years before the party

E ven when his desired transformation was more-or-less complete, Harris didn't let his new habits fall away. In fact, his feeling of vitality and energy was addictive, making him feel as if he could do anything, be anything, inserting a newfound confidence into his life, both socially and academically. He studied hard, *very* hard, and achieved grades higher than he ever had in his previous school, where he'd spent many of his classes daydreaming and doing the bare minimum. In spite of this discipline, he still made sure he had time for friends – indeed, his social life picked up and he found himself in a group of other boys – not exactly the popular crowd (or the *A-listers*, as he thought of them) but by no means at the lower end of the student hierarchy.

In the school holidays he had sleepovers, attended parties, even went away for a long weekend with his new friend, Ethan, and his parents to their villa in Monte Carlo. Both Isabelle and Patrick encouraged this, although Patrick was the only one who seemed to have any interest in what he got up to. If he ever tried to speak to Isabelle about what he was doing or where he'd be at a certain time, she always gave him a tight, half-smile (or no smile at all) and replied, 'That all sounds fine.'

The instance where Harris had caught Raphael looking at him from his doorway hadn't been repeated exactly, but as the weather improved and summer approached, leading to sunbathing and swimming outdoors, he still got the sense that he was being watched closer than he had been before. Raphael seemed to think there was safety in numbers and often crammed the house with school friends who, whilst not unkind to Harris, seemed content with following Raphael's lead of barely talking to him.

Things between the two boys weren't exactly ideal, but there had been a thawing of tension as the months had gone on and they had settled into a way of co-existing. Raphael was civil, polite even, if not exactly warm and friendly. But at the end of the academic year, marking half a year since he'd entered the Moncrieff's lives, something changed.

Harris had long been aware that Raphael's schoolwork wasn't going swimmingly. Both Isabelle and

Patrick had endeavoured to have 'serious conversations' about it, both with Raphael present and with each other in hushed tones when they thought neither of the boys could hear. One hot summer's day, though, it all blew up into a massive row.

'You drift through life thinking that being rich and beautiful is enough!' Isabelle shouted, and Harris heard from upstairs the sound of something breaking. 'Well maybe it used to be,' she continued, 'but I can promise you, it really isn't any more. I know what the world is like out there. And it is fierce, Raphael. Fierce and terrifying. And if you don't want to be seen as a failure among all your friends, and watch everyone else succeed while you lounge about doing fuck all, then you had better start doing some hard work.'

Harris moved to the landing and looked down. The argument seemed to be taking place in the kitchen. He listened some more, enough to hear Patrick, who often seemed to play the role of peacemaker, say something along the lines of 'I'm sure he'll work hard to catch up over the summer break.'

Then Harris heard approaching movement. He headed back into his room and heard the unmistakable shout of Raphael on the stairs. 'Well maybe you should find yourself another fucking son, then! Oh wait, you already did!'

Raphael went into his room and slammed the door with such violence that Harris felt his desk shake. He tried to carry on with what he was doing on his laptop but his mind wouldn't let go of the words he'd just heard booming across the landing. Amidst the grief of losing his parents, and his dislike of Raphael for making him feel so unwelcome, he'd never really thought about what it must have been like for Raphael to have a stranger thrust into his family. Someone who initially looked and sounded inferior – or Raphael's snobbish view of inferior – only to have that person steadily morph into something resembling a threat.

Although Harris didn't think there was any danger of Isabelle considering him as a son to rival Raphael, he nevertheless felt bad about what he had heard. He was surprised at his own feelings of sympathy and tried to dismiss them at first. But then remembered something his mother used to say when he was younger if boys had been mean to him in the playground: *Don't kick a bully when they're down, offer a helping hand and turn them into a friend.* This had worked when he was eight years old at school, so after thinking about it whilst pottering about his room for a couple of hours as night started to draw in, he gave in. He walked across the landing and did something he'd never done – nor had any wish to do – during his whole time at the Moncrieff's home. He knocked on Raphael's door. A simple act of kindness. One that would come to have far-reaching consequences in his life for years to come.

Chapter Fourteen

RAPHAEL

Three years before the party

'I don't want to talk anymore,' Raphael called out. He assumed his parents had returned to hassle him some more. He'd already agreed to do the programme of summer catch-up work the school had 'suggested' (code for 'insisted upon'). What more could they want from him? A repeat of his entire school life?

The door opened. He turned over, ready to start raging at either his mother or father, but he was surprised to find neither of them standing there. Instead, he saw Harris, slowly making his way into his bedroom.

'What are you doing in here?' he said, getting up off the bed. He was unsure how to respond and felt a pressing need to say something smart, snarky and highly intelligent. When nothing came he settled simply for, 'Get out of my room.'

Harris didn't do as instructed. Instead he walked into the main part of the room in the space between the window and the bed. Raphael saw him looking at the piles of books on the desk in the room. Papers scattered around, some folded into the books, some loose. The spines of the volumes un-dented. He felt he could see Harris's mind working, see the boy perhaps wondering how much his slipping grades was due to lack of intelligence and skill and how much was simply due to a lack of application. Raphael flattered himself it was the latter. As he watched Harris, he started to back away, feeling as though this strange and unprecedented invasion of his room was a sign of something sinister in the boy. Perhaps Harris planned to attack, to bring some sort of belated vengeance against him for all those tricks Raphael had played on him when he'd first come to live here.

Instead, Harris just sat down, uninvited, on Raphael's desk chair. He didn't say anything for a moment or two, shuffled his feet a bit, his socks making a slight rasping sound on the carpet. 'I thought I might be able to help.'

This was even more surprising to Raphael than if Harris had tried to hit him. 'Help? What do you mean?'

Harris seemed entirely calm. 'I mean help in the normal way people mean help.'

Raphael narrowed his eyes at him. 'There's nothing

normal about you,' he said in a low voice. 'You're ... *weird*.'

'That isn't kind. Or true,' Harris said, with no trace of offence or emotion. Indeed, his relaxed, unhurried manner was continuing to disconcert Raphael more than anything else. It was worse than if he'd started to shout or laugh or jeer. Raphael felt he was being attacked by stealth in a way, as though he had been thrown into a game he didn't know how to play.

'It *is* true. You ... you ... become an exercise fanatic, lose weight, start doing a thousand crunches or whatever to get those abs, actually go as far as to change your fucking voice so you now sound like a completely different person since you arrived – something nobody else seems to care about or notice.'

'Again, that's not true,' Harris said. 'People have noticed. They treat me better. Don't you think that's sad?'

'No, I don't,' Raphael said, feeling a rush of confidence, moving closer to his adopted brother. 'I find it *weird*.'

'I'm pleased you like my newly visible abs,' Harris said, leaning back, as if to show them off. He raised his shoulders. Raphael saw his T-shirt lift, showing an inch of his stomach area. It was hard and toned, just as he'd noticed before. And there was something in his expression that Raphael didn't like. Something a little too knowing. Any confidence Raphael had started to feel evaporated quickly and he took a step back.

'What...' he started to say, and his heart leapt, his pulse noticeably quickening.

Harris rolled his eyes. 'Calm down. I'm not here to wind you up. I just came to ask if you needed any help with your catch-up work. I could help you get back on track.'

Raphael couldn't properly compute what he was saying. 'I don't get why you're being so...'

'So what?'

'So nice?'

'I don't get why you haven't been so nice,' Harris said. 'Ever since I came here, ever since the first time I met you, spoke to you, you've never made me feel welcome.'

'That's because you're *not*!' Raphael said, almost shouting now.

Harris stood up. 'Sorry, but I didn't come here to be shouted at. I felt bad for you, that's all. I think you're unhappy, Raphael. For whatever reason, that's your business, but I just thought I could come and help.'

Raphael felt a surge of embarrassment rising within him and knew his face was probably burning red. 'I don't need your help. I'm in a different year than you, anyway. What makes you think you'd even know ... you'd even understand...'

'Test me,' Harris said. 'Give me one of your essays you have to do – or any assignment, really – and I'll get you an A. Perhaps an A* if we're both lucky.'

Raphael stared at him for a good few seconds. Then he turned away and reached for a piece of paper on his desk. 'Here you go. The Great Fucking Gatsby. Most boring book in the world.'

He watched as Harris read through the essay question at the top of the paper.

'Yeah, I can do this,' Harris said.

'Have you even read the book?'

Harris nodded. Then he gave Raphael a quick smile and headed for the door.

'Is that it?' Raphael asked.

'What more do you want? I'll do the essay tonight. Give it to you in the morning.'

Raphael clenched his jaw. 'I know why you're doing this. You think this will give you something over me.'

Harris just looked at him. Then said, 'Do you always think the worst of people?'

'Well if not that, then why?'

Harris was quiet for a moment, then he said, 'Because I don't feel I've ever been much use to anyone with my mind. Back in London, I did well in school but I never felt my teachers had much passion for what they taught. My parents praised my achievements when I did well, but ... well, I just never felt they really appreciated how clever I was. Does that sound arrogant to you?'

Raphael narrowed his eyes. 'Do you care what I think?'

Harris sighed. 'I'm trying to be emotionally open with

you, Raphael. Don't try to turn it into something combative. I'm telling you I'd quite like to feel wanted for something that I'm good at for the first time in my life.'

'Wanted? You want me to want your help?'

Harris said nothing. Just looked back at him. 'Fine,' Raphael said, raising his hands, 'you win. Just … no more talk of…'

'Talk of what?' Harris asked, his voice light and pleasant.

'Abs,' Raphael said, staring back at him. 'You understand?'

He watched as Harris raised his eyebrows. 'If you say so.' Then he was gone, leaving Raphael feeling both uneasy and confused about what had just happened.

The next day, Raphael woke to find a completed essay, typed on sheets of crisp stapled A4 paper, sitting on his desk. Five days after submitting it at school under his name, it was returned with an 'A*' grade in red pen in the top right-hand corner.

Chapter Fifteen

HARRIS

Three years before the party

For Harris, helping Raphael with his essay felt good. He felt as if the strange, icy silence between them both had started to thaw, and after his successful attempts to change his image and his accent, Harris's next focus – to improve his relationship with his adopted brother – was off to a good start. He was aware that Raphael suspected him of having ulterior motives and that this was part of some grand game he was playing, but Harris knew he was sincere in his attempts to help him, and that, in the end, was what really mattered. He'd been thrilled his initial effort had resulted in an A* grade and was confident that Raphael wouldn't be able to resist coming back for more assistance.

Perhaps, if he was truly honest with himself, he knew

he was playing something of a Machiavellian game, but it just wasn't the one Raphael suspected. It wasn't as though Harris desperately wanted to be part of Raphael's friendship circle, or that he needed another friend – he felt quite content with the ones he already had from school. It was more the challenge and the project of winning him over that intrigued him. He was fairly sure that he could do it. But it wasn't just the challenge that appealed to him. It was something deeper, more personal. A need to belong. He didn't kid himself that things would be perfect or ever feel completely right, but the animosity from Raphael had been the biggest barrier to Harris feeling settled and comfortable in this new family unit, so he hoped a thaw could take place between them. A gradual lessening of confrontation and resentment. Then, before long, maybe Raphael wouldn't treat him like an enemy or a cuckoo in the nest anymore. It would probably be too much to expect him to see Harris as a brother, but possibly a friend? Someone who he could get along with. Chat to. Surely that wasn't too much to ask.

Although Harris was pretty sure he had the measure of Raphael Moncrieff, he did succeed in surprising him one hot July evening. It was a week after the A* essay and Raphael came into Harris's room without warning, clutching something in his hands. Harris, who had been lying on his bed, headphones on and listening to music, enjoying the hint of a night-time breeze from the window, sat upright quickly when he spotted movement to his left.

'Hey,' Raphael said.

'You should knock,' said Harris, pausing the music he'd been listening to.

Raphael raised his eyebrows. 'Why? So you can hide your heroin? Brush away the cocaine?'

Harris wasn't amused by Raphael's clunky attempt at humour and sighed as he pulled himself up to a sitting position. 'Well there's no cocaine here. Sorry to disappoint. What do you want?'

Raphael stood in front of him, looking awkward. 'I just … just came to give you this.' He held out what he was holding. Harris took it. It was a book. A hardback. *The Great Gatsby*.

'I've … already got a copy,' Harris said, puzzled.

'I figured that,' Raphael said, 'but … well … the way you wrote about it in that essay. It made me think maybe I'd got the book wrong. And maybe … I thought … it seemed like you really liked it. From what you wrote, it seemed like it was important to you. You understood it way more than I ever had. So I got you a nice edition.'

Feeling rather stunned, Harris looked down at it. It was beautiful. It had gold, foil-coated lettering and an ornate border in cream and brown colours. And to Harris's surprise, he found he was close to tears. The unexpected nature of the gift had moved him. 'Thank you,' he said in a small voice.

Raphael sat down next to him. Although he hadn't been invited to do so, the act felt surprisingly natural, as did the closeness of his body.

'You're welcome,' he said. 'I'm sorry... I... I hope it hasn't upset you.'

Although there was no particular connection to the book and his parents, Harris suddenly couldn't stop thinking of every generous act they'd bestowed upon him, every moment of kindness. A present when he'd done well in a school report. A trip out with his dad to the cinema when he was allowed to get the expensive ice cream he wasn't usually allowed. The time he came home when he was eleven to find they'd both got him his own computer for him to do his homework on. It was as if those memories had suddenly been given oxygen, and he felt both happy and sad at the same time.

'It hasn't upset me, not really,' Harris said, self-consciously raising a hand to his eye to wipe away a stray tear.

'So why are you crying?' Raphael said. His voice was soft, curious sounding. Caring, even.

'I'm not crying,' said Harris, trying to move away, but Raphael took his arm. Not harshly, but still firmly in his grip, keeping Harris where he was.

'You are allowed to cry, you know,' he said.

'I know,' Harris replied in barely more than a whisper. The tears, however, had stopped and he took in a breath. He suddenly didn't feel sad anymore. There was something about the atmosphere in the room that had pulled him out of his moment of grief. Something electric. Dangerous, even. Impossible to ignore. He looked at Raphael. Raphael looked at him. Came closer to him. Said something in barely a whisper. 'Come to my room. Now.'

Harris found he didn't have much breath, as if there was a weight on his chest. 'Why your room?' he asked.

'Because it's further from my parents' room. And I don't want them to hear.' Raphael was still talking in a whisper, his face even closer.

'Hear what?' Harris asked, his heart beating fast.

Raphael didn't reply. He just took Harris's right hand in his and pulled him towards the door.

Harris woke up the next morning with the idea that something was out of place. He couldn't quite work it out, then realised that the computer on the table was different to his – the shoes by the bed looked too large. His duvet covers felt different. A few seconds later, he realised why. He wasn't in his room. And there was someone next to him.

Then he remembered everything.

The warm, sturdy frame of Raphael Moncrieff moved sleepily up against him, his chin settling on Harris's shoulder. He watched as Raphael's chest gently rose and fell with each breath, how his eyelids flickered, how his smooth, natural tan reflected the morning light shining through a chink in the curtains. Then his eyes opened. And Harris saw the panic.

'What the—' Raphael jerked up violently, looking at Harris with apparent terror. 'Oh … fuck,' he said, putting his head in his hands, fingers pressing into his eyes, as if he were attempting to wipe away any memories of the night before. 'You … you need to go,' he said, his voice even deeper than usual, croaky with sleep.

'Are … you okay?' Harris asked, pulling himself up in the bed.

'I said, fucking *go*,' Raphael replied, lowering his hands, his eyes red, angry looking, perhaps near tears.

'It's okay,' Harris said, 'I won't tell anyone…'

'Of course you won't fucking tell anyone,' Raphael hissed, getting out of bed, pulling the duvet away from Harris. 'Because if you do… I'll…' He looked around him wildly, struggling to find the words, 'I'll … go to the fucking police.'

Harris froze. 'What? What are you talking about? We … we didn't do anything wrong.'

'*You* fucking did,' Raphael said, and Harris could see his hands trembling as he hurriedly started to dress, tugging on some boxers and scrabbling around for a T-shirt from the clothes on the floor. 'If you ever speak … *ever* tell anyone about … well … I'll tell them you made me. That you … you…' He looked around at his surroundings then dived at the desk, picking something up off it. 'That you threatened me with this!' He threw the object at Harris. It landed near his left arm and he picked it up, confused. It was a large penknife, the sort he'd imagine forest workers or explorers would use. He didn't know why Raphael had such a thing or why he was now throwing it at him, but as he held it in his hands he saw something close to triumph in the boy's eyes.

'There, you've touched it.' He reached forward and grabbed it back. 'Your fingerprints are on it now.' He dropped it into a half-open desk drawer and then closed it.'

'You're not serious,' Harris said. 'That doesn't ... I wouldn't ... I really don't think—'

'Just shut up ... fucking shut up,' Raphael said, his face now pained, his hands clutching at his short hair. 'I'll tell them you tried it on with me ... tried to ...you know ... and then they'll get rid of you. You'll be sent away to a fucking children's home or something. Or you'll end up on the streets. Mum and Dad won't keep you here. They won't. Not if ... not if they knew what you tried to do to me. I'll say you came in here and started touching me, telling me if I didn't let you fuck me you'd ... you'd kill me and everyone else in the house. They'll think you're a fucking psycho. Even if they can't prove it, they'll always wonder, won't they? You'll never be one of the family after that. You'll be the weird psycho kid who might murder them in their sleep because you want to fuck their son. They'll hate you.'

Harris was so horrified and astonished by this, he found he couldn't speak. So he just got up and started to pull on his clothes and went to leave the room. He travelled along the landing in a daze. Once in his bedroom, he sat in his chair, looking out of the window for a long time, thinking. He hadn't been exactly surprised when, the night before, Raphael had leaned in to kiss him. He'd kissed a few girls before, at some parties with friends, and had never really thought about kissing a boy, but he'd guessed that was what Raphael secretly liked. So he'd gone along with it, and found he didn't mind the idea of getting into bed with him. Raphael had been gentle at first, then something else had taken over, a rougher edge, like some primal energy had been unlocked within him. Harris thought he understood why this was and found it quite excited him – to be the one who brought an intense, passionate side out of an otherwise sullen, confused, repressed young man. Raphael hadn't talked during it, nor afterwards as they lay silent and breathing heavily in the darkness before sleep took them both. There had been a moment in the night when he'd woken and thought he'd heard Raphael crying, very gently, next to him, but he'd been in that strange hinterland between sleep and wakefulness and wasn't sure at the time if it was real or if he'd been dreaming.

The reaction he'd been greeted with that morning had surprised him, but after a good half hour of pondering he realised how well it fitted his adopted brother's character. A tough, strong, handsome, rich boy, terrified of showing the world any weakness – or something he incorrectly perceived as a weakness.

As he sat in his seat, thinking, Harris heard the sound of the shower running, then a door open and then closing. Steps on the landing proceeded the quiet, careful opening of his door. Raphael entered.

'Have you come to threaten me some more?' Harris asked, not getting up.

Raphael folded his arms, looking surly. He'd changed into a short-sleeved polo top and khaki shorts. Both emphasised his strength and muscles. No matter how much work and strength training Harris had done over the past months, he was still pretty sure Raphael would beat him in a fight with ease.

'I just came to say … I want you to carry on. Helping me. With the essays, I mean, and the rest of the catch-up work over the summer.'

Harris would have laughed if he hadn't felt so disorientated. 'You're joking, right? After that? After that little strop you pulled in there, after all those horrible things you said, those threats… Why should I help you? Why should I ever talk to you ever again?'

Raphael stood very straight-backed, as if height would give him the courage to say whatever he was going to say next. 'You do that, you carry on helping me, and I won't … I won't tell them you forced me. I won't say any of those things.'

Harris stared at him for a few seconds before saying 'Fine'. Then he turned away from him to face his desk and opened his computer.

He heard Raphael go to leave the room, but before he'd passed through the doorway, Harris said, quietly, 'I would have helped you anyway, you know. Before you said all those things. Before we did what we did last night. If you'd have asked, I'd have helped.'

Raphael paused. Although Harris couldn't see him, he could hear his breathing. But he didn't respond. Just left the room, leaving Harris feeling hurt, unsettled and sad.

Chapter Sixteen

HARRIS

The day of the party

Harris sees Raphael extracting himself from a group that includes Lauren's parents and two other people he doesn't recognise. He comes over and says 'Harris, can we talk?'

He ushers the younger man round the side of the house. For a moment, Harris thinks they're going to go into the greenhouses again but Raphael takes a sharp left down a path that Harris knows comes out to a slope where a bench is set amidst some trees. A little ornamental fountain tinkles away, giving the area a calming feel. Raphael, however, looks the opposite of calm.

'You okay?' asks Harris.

'No I am bloody not okay,' he says. 'Why... What you

said earlier … why did you have to go bringing up that … that error of mine. It was years ago and we've moved on since and now, at my wedding, you—'

'I thought this was an engagement party, not a wedding,' says Harris, blankly.

'Don't give me that, you know what I mean. I … I've struggled, okay. Struggled with … many things. Many feelings. It's not easy, you know… You seem able to flit between whoever you want to and that's bloody great for you. But … it hasn't been so easy for me. And I have a constant guilt about it.'

This little outburst takes Harris by surprise. 'So you're saying … what? *Sorry*? Sorry for sleeping with me once, then feeling so bad about it that you tell me never to speak of it and then even go as far as blackmailing me into silence? You had me do so much of your school work and I probably don't have to point this out, but it's still going on. I'm still helping you out with your uni work like it's become some bloody habit—'

'Oh, I don't think of that as … well, part of what happened,' Raphael says, flapping a hand at Harris, 'that's entirely separate.'

'Do you think I'm still writing essays for you for *fun*?'

Raphael looks strained, perhaps on the verge of tears. 'No, because … well … because you care about me. Just like I care about you.'

Harris frowns. This isn't how he expected this

conversation to go. He'd wondered if Raphael would kick off about the little jibe earlier, but he'd intended it to unsettle him, to create a feeling and general atmosphere of unease and dread for him. He hadn't expected it to cause some emotional semi-confession unravelling. 'Is that all you want to apologise for?' he asks, staring back at him.

'What? Yes ... I ... do ... I *am* sorry.'

Harris waits a moment. It doesn't seem like Raphael is about to say anything further. For a few seconds, all Harris can hear are the sounds of the trees swaying above them, the vague hum of conversation from the guests a short distance away, and the drops and gushes from the fountain. In spite of this ambient noise, the world seems to pause for a brief, strange moment. Then someone calls out, 'Raphy?'

Lauren comes into view, looking confused. 'Raphy. What are you doing? My father saw you sneaking off with Harris. He thought you were going to have a smoke, but I told him that was nonsense and that we'd agreed smoking was something weak people did and it was offensive to anyone who had ever lost a relative through cancer, whether smoking-related or otherwise.'

When Raphael doesn't say anything to this, Lauren prompts, 'Don't you agree?'

'Yes. No. I mean, yes that's right.' Raphael bites his lip, blinks quickly, then turns to face his fiancée. 'Sorry, darling, I just ... I wanted to talk to Harris. He and my father had a disagreement recently and I wanted to check he was all right.'

Harris thinks he sees a flash of understanding in Lauren's face – an odd look that suggests what she is hearing isn't entirely news to her. It's gone in an instant, though, and she says 'I'm so sorry to hear about that. Family quarrels can be … stressful, can't they?'

'Yes, they can be,' Harris says, allowing his eyes to flick to Raphael, before returning to Lauren.

Lauren smiles at him. 'But at least it sounds like you've mended things now. May I ask – if this isn't terribly rude of me – how the disagreement broke out?'

'My father's giving Harris a house,' Raphael says, 'but he says Harris may not want it.'

'That isn't entirely true,' Harris replies, frowning at Raphael. 'I suppose, maybe, in some sense it is. But there's … a bigger picture to it all. And the house is quite far away. In Essex.'

Lauren looks puzzled. 'Well, that's … good. And Essex can be lovely … I think. I haven't really been there, but it's not so very far. Only a few hours, and Raphy and I would be certain to visit, wouldn't we?'

Raphael nods, not looking at Harris.

'I think Raphy knows some people who were originally from Essex, is that right? The Hammonds? Arnold Hammond and his wife … I forget her name.'

'They're from Kent,' Raphael replies bluntly.

'Oh … perhaps it was Alfred and Katherine?'

'Alfred's from London.'

'Oh, I've heard of Alfred,' Harris says. 'He's the one who works in covert surveillance technologies. Fascinating job.'

He sees Raphael's head jerk up sharply as he says this, but Lauren sweeps on and Harris keeps his attention directed her way.

'Yes, very. But in terms of the house thing, I really don't think you need to fall out about it. And besides, many people would simply dream of being handed a house at ... well, such a young age. That really is ... very interesting.'

Harris stares back at her unblinking. 'I promise you, Lauren, this isn't about being grateful or ungrateful. There's more to it than that.'

Raphael's eyes have returned to him and Harris can tell he is becoming more interested in the subject. He opens his mouth, apparently about to ask a question, when he's stopped by the sound of a new addition to the group.

'Here you all are,' Isabelle says, stopping by the fountain and looking around at everyone. Her eyes narrow, perhaps suspecting there's something odd afoot. 'Why are you three gathered over here away from all the guests? Raphael, I've just been talking to Tabitha and William Delargy, the twins you knew from playschool, and they are *dying* to say hello to you – it's been years since you saw them. Come back with me and we'll find them.' She raises a hand, and for a second Harris thinks she's about to click her fingers at her son, but instead she settles for a beckoning motion and then adds, 'I'm sure they'd love to meet you, too, Lauren, dear.' She says nothing to Harris – barely gives him a cursory glance, before turning to go back to the party. This would have bothered him once, but today he contents himself with the knowledge that very soon, Isabelle won't be able to take her eyes off him.

Part II

THE CRIMES OF ISABELLE MONCRIEFF

Chapter Seventeen

ISABELLE

The day of the party

I sabelle has done her very best, as the day has gone on, not to let the mix-up with the chair delivery upset her. She's always had trouble putting things aside that annoy her – they have a habit of clouding her entire horizon. Focus is something she's always prided herself on – being able to concentrate on a task and follow it to its conclusion, provided she has the right mindset – but she's long been aware that if annoyance or anger sneaks into the mix, she'll find it very hard to keep her attention in check. Today has, so far, been a success, incorrect chairs aside. There was also a tense moment when it looked as though the screens in the garden wouldn't work, when a distorted and stretched picture of Lauren and Raphael filled the glass expanse and wouldn't budge, the distorted image giving Lauren a manic sort of look that would probably have unsettled the guests if it had remained. But some tweaking later, they'd got the photo presentation working. Isabelle had always thought the whole idea of having photos displayed of the two of them on screens outside was a preposterous idea and more than a little tacky. This wasn't even their wedding day, after all. But she got the feeling Lauren needed to have an idea that was very much 'hers' and something she could mastermind, so Isabelle had decided it was easier to pick her battles.

During the first hour of the garden party she mingles and smiles and tries to avoid the occasional probing question from her guests (such as how brief her son's engagement is set to be). She nips these in the bud with practised brief mentions of 'young love' and 'impossible to overrule the youth of today' – ignoring the fact that her future daughter-in-law, who is eighteen months off thirty, is no longer really a youth. Some of the conversations Isabelle enjoys and she sees friends she hasn't bumped into for a while. She is actively pleased to see Elena Ashton, with whom she went to school, and Elena's daughter, Pippa. Elena alludes to her divorce of a few years back and Isabelle makes sympathetic facial expressions, then asks Pippa how she is doing. The young woman – extremely pretty, wearing a vibrant red dress – tells her she too is engaged to be married, and is currently a columnist for a right-of-centre website.

'What are you working on at the moment?' Isabelle asks.

'Immigration. The website is US based, but I offer a British slant on a lot of issues. So at the moment it's a lot about immigrants coming over here and what that means for our society.'

Isabelle notices Elena looking troubled. 'And do you have much experience in immigration or the areas involved in monitoring the issue?' she asks, guessing the answer.

'Oh, no,' Pippa says. 'It's just my thoughts and concerns. That's not the only topic, though. I write about loads of other things. Like the more bizarre parts of our culture at the moment, the progressive left gone mad, that sort of thing. And all the climate-change stuff. Governments making individuals feel guilty about using their own cars whilst messing up all the business deals themselves. What's really helpful is that there are now a bunch of topics that people on both the right and the left generally agree upon, but the left are scared stiff of admitting they agree so stay silent and pretend they don't agree, but the right has the courage to stand up and shout. That's why websites like the one I work for end up getting all the traffic from both sides. Not that the lefties would admit to reading it. It's rather fun, watching all the virtue-signallers tear themselves to pieces over it all.'

'Indeed,' Isabelle says, unsure how to politely unpack everything that has just been mentioned.

'I agree,' says a voice to her left. She turns and is surprised to see Harris standing there, holding a wine glass, smiling at them all. 'I think there's a whole lot of stuff that's nuts about the progressive left these days. Especially when a lot of the nonsense they come out with is spouted by the rich and privileged.'

'Oh, gosh, I completely agree,' says Pippa animatedly. 'Like the ones who are apparently in love with free speech then go suddenly deaf when one of their friends is torn apart for an ill-judged joke they made years ago. Or dare to speak their minds and then are made to go on some ghastly apology circus where they talk endlessly about how they're "listening" and "learning". Or when they care oh-so-much about the environment and the planet and the cute little dolphins and starfish and then take forty-seven helicopters to their film sets.' She lets out a laugh, and Harris laughs, too.

'Exactly,' says Harris, nodding. 'Do you know, I think Hollywood actors are some of the most hypocritical of all, these days.'

'Absolutely,' says Pippa. 'Gosh, this has given me a really good idea for an article, actually.' She laughs. 'Hollywood Hypocrisy Gone Mad. Something like that. It's all so ridiculous. I think people just say what they think they should be saying so as not to jeopardise their next job.'

'Completely,' Harris says. 'Wouldn't you agree, Isabelle?' He turns to look at her.

'Er...' Isabelle looks taken aback. 'I should formerly introduce you... This is Harris, my ... he's ... we adopted him a few years ago... Harris, this is Helena, an old school friend of mine, and her daughter, Pippa.'

'You've worked with Hollywood actors, Isabelle,' Harris continues, as if her awkward introductions haven't happened. 'A lot of them, I believe. Tell us, are they all so nauseatingly pious in real life?'

Isabelle feels herself growing more tense with each passing second. 'I ... well ... some of them, perhaps.'

'I've only ever met one Hollywood actor,' Harris says, taking a large sip from his drink.

With a stab of horror, Isabelle's fears about where this might be going are confirmed. 'Harris, could you come and give me a hand with the chairs.'

'I'm trying to think of her name... Ah, yes, Natasha Crewe,' Harris says, raising a finger in the air. 'That's the one. Interesting woman.'

'Harris,' Isabelle prompts again, aware the note of warning in her voice must now be very audible.

'Yes, I've heard tons of rumours about her,' says Pippa, nodding, in a semi-conspiratorial way, 'really juicy ones, too.'

'And I bet all of them are true,' Harris says, also nodding, his expressions exaggerated. Isabelle sees his eyes flick over to her.

'Yes, that's all rather interesting,' Isabelle says, somewhat hurriedly. 'Come on, Harris.' She grabs his arm and tries to turn him around. 'Nice to see you, Helena. Pippa.' She nods at them both and succeeds in dragging Harris away. He comes with her, waving at the two confused-looking women as they depart.

'What on earth's got into you?' Isabelle hisses once they are safely round the side of the house away from the guests.

Harris does a look of mock shock, his eyes wide. 'Oh, gosh, was I *indiscreet*? Is Natasha here?' He makes a show of looking around, then smirks. 'Maybe I should say hello, if she is. You know, catch up on old times.'

He then walks off before Isabelle can say anything. She watches, feeling shaken and horrified, as the boy wanders back in the direction of the guests. Smiling and saying hello to people. Putting on the charm. Potentially telling them anything.

Chapter Eighteen

ISABELLE

Two years before the party

Natasha Crewe was Isabelle's idea. The film she and her colleagues had been working on was in danger of floundering, and Natasha was their ticket out of the 'flounder stage'. Isabelle had put in a huge amount of time and effort to make sure her company excelled, ever since Patrick had agreed to finance her attempt to make it in the industry alone. It had worked. More than worked, and over time she had built up a reputation as a problem solver. A miracle worker. A woman with instinct and connections. Someone filmmakers and studios wanted working for them. But in spite of all of this, it wasn't uncommon to inherit some 'problem projects' – indeed, these were often the films Isabelle found the most interesting to work on. But this particular project in question had been bubbling along with little progress for too long, hence the fears of a 'flounder stage' setting in. In fact, one could have realistically argued it was already there, and that the Natasha idea saved it from going into the 'development hell' stage. The studio was keen, as were Isabelle's team. 'She's totally right for the role,' said her two employees, Susannah and Craig, almost at the same time, when she mentioned the idea on one of their Zoom calls. Isabelle generally liked them both, although wasn't always convinced they worked well together. Susannah was British, but had been educated in the US, then had returned to go to Cambridge University. She spoke with a mid-Atlantic accent, was coolly efficient in a way Isabelle admired greatly, but had a habit of biting off people's heads if they rubbed her up the wrong way. Craig was American, from New York City, had worked for ten years in the production arm of a nascent streaming service before hopping over to the UK. Isabelle wasn't entirely sure if he had settled into her business quite yet, but she decided to give him a bit more time to prove himself before she considered letting him go.

'Natasha is really good at what she does. And all that stuff – that chatter about her – has all blown away now,' said Susannah.

'Yeah, she's not on any red lists as far as I know,' Craig added. 'I mean, shagging teenage pop stars when you're hurtling towards forty isn't the worst thing – shows she's got some life in her yet.'

'People were probably just pouncing on it to fill column inches or the sidebar of shame,' Susannah agreed. 'Gossip sells. The world carries on. And that boy band member was, like, sixteen or seventeen wasn't he? Perfectly fine.'

'Yeah, if anything, I think those judging her were being a bit misogynistic,' said Craig.

'Totally,' said Susannah, nodding.

'Although, I suppose if she was a guy people would have still called it a bit ... creepy,' said Craig, pulling a face.

'You just said it was fine,' said Isabelle. 'How can it be creepy and fine at the same time?'

'It can't be,' said Susannah.

'It *can*,' said Craig. 'One person's creepy is another person's *hell, yes*! But the point still stands. People would have still come for her if she were a guy. It's just the language and insults would have been different. That's the nuance.'

Susannah's expression grew more irritated. 'But you just said it was misogyny that people *did* criticise her,' said Susannah. 'So what would it have been if she was a guy? Misandrist? You do know that misandry doesn't really exist, Craig? It's a bullshit theory cooked up by incels on Reddit.'

This resulted in an outraged look from Craig. 'I can't figure out if you're being satirical, Susannah, or just tragically misinformed – I'm truly lost,' he said, holding his hands in his air, the Zoom image freezing then jerking for a second making it look like he was performing a random dance move.

'Shall we get back to the subject in hand,' said Isabelle, used to the fiery personalities of her two workers but reluctant to let this descend into a sixth-form debate club spat.

'Natasha's in London next week,' said Susannah. 'We could approach her agent? Set up a meeting?'

'How do you know that?' asked Craig.

'It's my business to know. I bother to read the industry press. I make notes. Remember things. I shouldn't have to apologise for doing my homework, Craig.' Her tone was still snippy so Isabelle raised an eyebrow, leaning back from the laptop to show she wasn't pleased. 'Anyway, uh, well,' Susannah continued, now sounding sheepish, 'she only ever stays at the Rallton or Claridge's. Since the pandemic, it's been more the latter.'

'Why, what did the Rallton do wrong?' asked Craig.

'Empty hand sanitiser station in the main lobby,' Susannah replied with a sigh. 'Natasha had a meltdown. Someone filmed it on their phone and put it on TikTok, set it to music. The theme tune to *The Archers*, if I remember rightly.'

'Natasha played a recurring character on that show back when she did a lot of British radio in the nineties,' Craig said very quickly. 'A nymphomaniac bovine specialist. It must have been a reference to that.'

'Yes I got that, Craig,' said Susannah.

'Claridge's it is, then,' Isabelle said, making another valiant attempt to keep things on track.

'Shall I reach out to her agent, Isabelle, or would you like to?' Susannah asked, 'and is lunch okay?'

'Yes, an informal lunch at Claridge's or somewhere similar would be ideal. But I'll reach out to Dodie, her agent. I know him. *And* I know Natasha has been considering firing him – he told me as much – but while he still represents her let's keep him on side.'

Eight days later, Isabelle was sitting at a table in the restaurant at Claridge's enjoying its finest afternoon tea, with Natasha Crewe on one side and her agent Dodie Braythorne on the other. Natasha, who had a reputation within the industry of being all smiles and politeness to press and PR, but neurotic, paranoid and unpredictable behind the scenes (aside from the occasional public 'meltdown'), had been generally very agreeable, but hadn't committed one way or the other in terms of the film Isabelle was hoping to sign her for. When Natasha had agreed to meet but asked for the director, Jerry McFiece, who was attached to the project not to be present, Isabelle had been ready for a fight. So far the fight had not come, even when she tentatively asked why the director wasn't invited.

'I find him boring,' Natasha said, waving a hand and laughing to herself. 'Oh, Jerry's all right. I did a low-budget thriller with him back in the mid noughties. We were in … New Mexico, that was it. I think. Or it might have been Spain. Anyway, it was when I was very young and naïve and he was kind, but my God did he go on and on. I was surprised to hear he was attached to this, especially since he seems to have got a bit lost in the TV and movie world of late. A lot of I-shagged-a-psycho-stalker dramas for Lifetime. And I think he did a Christmas movie for Hallmark – something about a pony sanctuary, wasn't it? I mean, he's competent, sure, in a lets-get-this-done sort of way. He's just a bit yawn-inducing as an on-set presence. But I suppose I'll have to speak to him if I agree to do it. I just want contact to be kept to a minimum.' She took a bite of a scone. 'My God, this is delicious. If one more fucking gossip website implies I never eat carbs, I'm going to reference these cakes in the lawsuit as evidence that I live off stuff like this.' She dabbed at her lips with her napkin. 'So – tell me, rest of the cast. Anyone good? I thought the old lady who lives in the same apartment as the leads – that could totally go to one of the Dames? I have *longed* to work with Judi. Or Maggie. Or Eileen. Is Vanessa a Dame?'

Isabelle smiled. 'We're hoping for a notable name for

that. We're just checking scheduling conflicts with *Call the Midwife*.'

'And for the male co-star?'

'Jacques Garnier, I believe,' said Isabelle.

Natasha dropped her fork with a clatter. 'Absolutely not.'

Isabelle was taken aback. 'Sorry?'

'I detest that man. *Detest*.'

'Right,' said Isabelle, nodding slowly, taking in the sudden strong reaction. 'Can I ask—'

'You certainly can. He's a cunt.'

Isabelle thought she could feel the expletive echoing around the Claridge's tearoom as if someone had just fired a gun.

'I'm sorry to say it, but that man ... he ruined... *I* was in love with him. I was ... completely...'

'Oh, I'm so sorry,' said Isabelle, mortified. 'I had no idea you and he had been in a relationship.'

'I wasn't in a relationship with *him*,' said Natasha, her eyes wide, staring at Isabelle as if she were insane. 'Christ no, give me some credit. No, I was in a relationship with Evan Winscott.'

'The singer?' asked Isabelle, attempting to piece together what Natasha was trying to say.

'Yes, the fucking singer. I loved him, he loved me, or I thought he did. He was ... a bit younger than I am ... but it was perfectly ... um ... legal ... in most countries... And well, I caught him in a cupboard on a film set with

Jacques bloody Garnier. *Together*. I was horrified. Shaken to my very soul. My mind was shattered, my heart torn apart. It was like … like…' She cast wildly around with her hand, her face taut with theatrical anguish, and Isabelle was strongly reminded of the fact she was dining with an actress who had started her professional life at the RSC. 'It was like that line from Tennyson. *"Out flew the web and floated wide; The mirror crack'd from side to side; The curse is come upon me, cried The Lady of Shalott."'* She paused a moment, presumably to allow the impact of this literary reference to sink in, then added 'It *was* a curse. I thought Evan and I had a future. I was wrong. So very wrong.'

'Right,' said Isabelle again, 'I see how that might be … difficult.'

'So if you think I'm going to spend one moment breathing the same oxygen as that nasty, that awful, that…' Words at last seemed to fail Natasha, and she got up from the table, threw her napkin down on the table and left the room.

'There we go,' said Dodie in a resigned sort of way. 'I didn't think we'd get to a tea refill before she flounced out. God, I'm sick of her. This whole job is fucking awful. Why do I do, this, Isabelle? I'm sixty now and I'm pretty sure I have high blood pressure, and if I do, it's because of her. I wish she'd hurry up and fire me. If she doesn't, I might retire just to be shot of all this nonsense.' He rolled his eyes at Isabelle. 'Bloody actors. I wish I'd gone into banking like my father. My brother has a side project in breeding rabbits. I might go into that.' He leaned forward for the teapot on the table. 'Would you like some more?'

'I'll go and find her,' said Isabelle, standing up. Dodie nodded and waved a hand in a suit-yourself gesture.

After checking the ladies, Isabelle eventually found Natasha sat in the hotel foyer on one of the sofas in the corner, sunglasses over her eyes, even though she was still indoors and it was a rainy day. She was tapping on her phone and only looked up when Isabelle came right up close to her.

'Sorry,' she mumbled, 'got a bit … carried away.' She sniffed, felt around her pocketless dress, apparently looking for a tissue. Isabelle held a fresh one out from her bag. Natasha took it with a nod.

'Let's go back to the table and have a chat about how we could make working with Jacques a more … bearable prospect.'

Natasha started to protest but was interrupted by someone coming up to them and saying, 'Oh, there you are.'

Isabelle turned round to see Harris standing beside her.

'What are you doing here?' she asked, thoroughly confused. In her mind, the boy was back home in Bath, probably doing homework, or weights, or running, or whatever it was he got up to when unsupervised.

'I was in London. Wanted to go shopping. Patrick

said it was fine, and he mentioned you were in London and to message you so I could get a lift home rather than taking the train. Which I did, but got no reply. He said he thought you were going to be having a meeting here, so I decided to chance it.'

'You decided to interrupt a work meeting?' Isabelle said, her mouth going tight. She saw Harris's eyes flick to the distressed film star sitting in front of them and back to Isabelle, as if to say *This is a work meeting?* – sceptisism that Isabelle couldn't help but sympathise with. None of this was going to plan. She started to say that if Harris needed a lift he could find a quiet corner and wait until she was finished, but was stopped by Natasha. She rose from her chair and pulled off her sunglasses, peering at Harris as if she had never seen a teenage boy before – as if a rare animal had just scampered out of a forest and she wished to be the first to admire it. 'My, my, who do we have here, Isabelle? This can't be your son, can it?'

'No,' said Isabelle. 'Harris lives with us. We … took him in. When his parents sadly died. I … er … I'm not sure why he's here right now, though.'

Natasha nodded. 'I see.' She extended a hand to Harris, who shook it.

'Hey,' he said. 'Sorry, didn't recognise you with the shades on. I've seen you in films.'

Natasha did a light tinkling sort of laugh. 'Goodness, flattery will get you everywhere young man.' She stepped forward and came closer to Harris – close enough to smell the boy's aftershave. 'Do you have a favourite?'

'Er, a favourite what?' Harris asked, looking slightly afraid.

'A favourite film of mine.' Natasha's eyes, which had been red and puffy moments before, seemed to be returning to their normal piercing gaze with surprising rapidity.

When Harris didn't answer, Isabelle cleared her throat and said, 'Well, all your performances are amazing, Natasha, so who could possibly say?'

'I liked your version of *Great Expectations*,' Harris suddenly said. 'You were a great Estella. Really ... natural.'

Natasha beamed. 'Gosh, I'd quite forgotten that. I so rarely do television drama now. That must have been ten years ago. You must have been, what, five or six when that was on?'

Harris nodded. 'Yeah. But I streamed it, not long ago.'

Natasha nodded slowly. 'Gosh, to think of you, crouched over your laptop in your bedroom, watching something I made when you were just a little boy.'

Isabelle wasn't sure she liked the direction or tone of this conversation, so she cleared her throat again, saying 'Shall we return to the table and talk the contract through?'

Natasha turned to her, an expression of surprise and

confusion on her face, as if she'd forgotten why Isabelle was there. 'Oh, yes, perhaps…'

'Good,' Isabelle nodded. 'Stay here, Harris – I'll come and find you when it's time to leave.'

She led the way back, but couldn't help noticing how Natasha kept glancing back towards Harris. They skirted around a family with travel bags who had spotted a famous YouTuber and had successfully cornered him in an alcove near the lifts.

Later on, Isabelle wasn't entirely sure if the idea had crossed her mind at that point. Or if it came from further hints and allusions Natasha made in the communication between them after that day's meeting. But something stuck in her head from that moment on. A seed of possibility. Perhaps the boy her husband had forced into their lives might be more useful than she had originally thought.

Chapter Nineteen

HARRIS

Two years before the party

Harris was organising books in the library when Isabelle walked in. It had been Patrick's idea, to give some sense of order to the place. He had suggested sorting by genre, with Harris doing the categorising, helped by online bookstore pages, which he had open on the iMac that stood on the writing desk at the far side of the room.

Isabelle hadn't shown the slightest interest in the project, so when she walked in while Harris was in the midst of ordering all of Sue Grafton's 'alphabet' thrillers, he didn't attempt to involve her in the process. The best approach with Isabelle, he had found over the past eighteen months, was to interact only when needed.

'When you've finished with that and have a moment,

there's something I need to talk to you about,' she said. She took a seat in one of the armchairs, making it abundantly clear the 'moment' was now, whether Harris had finished or not.

'Er, okay,' Harris replied, setting down the pile of hardbacks on a step stool and taking a seat in one of the other chairs.

'We're going to America,' she said, simply.

Harris raised his eyebrows. 'We, as in…?'

'You and me,' she said.

Harris hadn't been expecting this. He was used to being home with just Isabelle when Patrick was on work trips and Raphael was out with friends or university, but they didn't exactly *do things* together. They just co-existed. The most they had travelled in each other's country was when she gave him a lift home from somewhere. To go jetting off across the world was a completely foreign proposition.

'Why?' he asked. He thought he saw something in Isabelle's face for a moment – like a small twitch or a moment of tension. But a split-second later it was gone.

'Well, I thought you could do with a holiday. You spend too much time in the house. I know you have your friends, but you've never been as sociable as Raphael, and Patrick and I are worried you're becoming too reclusive. So it's agreed. I need to go to Los Angeles for work and you are to come with me and … well … see the sights.'

'On my own?' Harris frowned. 'I'll be, what, drifting along the streets of LA while you work? I thought you needed to work here? I was going to stay here while you work and Patrick was going to take Raphael skiing?'

'That's still the case. But I now need to do my work in the US. Just for a week, if that, if it all goes well.'

Harris still wasn't clear about this sudden change of plan. When he didn't say anything, Isabelle said 'Surely you don't want to stay here alone?'

'I could.'

She shook her head, a little too harshly, causing her earrings to flash in the sunlight from the window. 'No, no. That wouldn't be … wouldn't be right.'

'I am seventeen. And Emmeline would be here, wouldn't she?'

'It's decided. You're to come with me to the States.' She got up. 'We leave tomorrow.'

'Tomorrow?' Harris protested, 'but I'm going to the centre of Bath with some friends tomorrow.'

'Rearrange it, for goodness sake,' Isabelle said, flicking her hand in the air with irritation. 'You could be a touch more grateful, Harris. Not every teenager gets a first class trip to LA handed to them on a platter. Go upstairs and pack, or I'll get Emmeline to do it for you.'

She left, leaving Harris sitting in the room alone. He was surprised to notice he felt glad. Glad that Isabelle wanted to spend time with him – or at least seemed to. Perhaps she had resolved to treat him more like a member of the family. Maybe she even felt regret, he wondered, as he went to pack. Regret at making him feel like an outsider to be tolerated. But as he took out a pile of folded T-shirts from his drawer and laid them in his travel case, he couldn't shake off another feeling. The sense that something odd was going on. He could just feel it.

Chapter Twenty

HARRIS

Two years before the party

Aside from a brief trip to France with the Moncrieffs the year before – and a cheap, package holiday to Spain with his parents many years before that – Harris hadn't really travelled abroad. Certainly never as far as America.

Isabelle barely spoke to him on the way to the airport or in the first class lounge, which was normal and to be expected from her, though disappointing. His hopes that this was her attempt to mend bridges – or at least build bridges that had never really been there in the first place – were quickly proving fruitless. It wasn't long before Harris found the length of time in her company a little difficult to get used to. Normally there'd either be someone else there to interrupt them, or he'd be able to go off to his room, whereas travelling across the world together meant experiencing – or enduring – her cold, near-silent demeanour for longer than was entirely comfortable. Nevertheless, he valiantly tried to keep the tone light, telling her how much he liked the yoghurt he'd chosen at the lounge buffet counter, or how comfortable his seat was on the plane when they boarded.

'You're talking a lot more than usual,' she remarked with a sigh as she sat down.

'Is … that bad?' Harris asked, unsure if she was criticising him or just making one of her typical blunt observations. He saw her glance behind her, perhaps wishing they'd been given pods in single-file, rather than next to each other.

'Not necessarily,' she said, taking off her sunglasses and putting them into her handbag. She then turned her head to look at him, her eyes narrowed, as if she was considering something. 'In fact, it's good you've been coming out of your shell over this past year,' she said, 'you're growing into a very … well, a nice young man.'

Harris would have been less surprised if she'd produced a gun from her Prada bag and fired it at his head. Ever since meeting her, she'd never once offered him a compliment – he got the feeling he didn't qualify for such a level of attention. Stunned, it took him a while to realise he was staring at her with his mouth open. Before he'd had a chance to respond (although how he was to do so hadn't quite come to him) Eleanor continued.

'So I hope you'll use your newfound confidence and ... um ... personable nature if we decide to socialise with anyone whilst in LA.' She averted her eyes at this point, busying her hands with the blanket and slipper packs that were set out to the side of each first class seat. She stowed hers away and took out a bottle of antibacterial gel and gave her hands a dousing. This was followed by a small quantity of very luxurious-looking hand cream.

Harris watched all this, still unsure how to reply. In the end, he just settled for 'Sure,' and shifted himself around, certain now that he had been correct and there was another aspect to their trip he hadn't been fully briefed on.

When they reached Los Angeles, Isabelle was in a prickly mood, informing him she had 'a killer of a headache' and that she needed to sleep. It wasn't even 3pm in the afternoon, local time, making it before 11pm in the UK, and Harris didn't feel like sleeping. So while Isabelle took to her room, he explored the hotel. He had a large burger in the restaurant, charging it all to Isabelle's booking account, and then discovered that the swimming pool, sauna and gym facilities were open 24-hours for hotel guests. Feeling motivated to burn off some of the calories he'd just consumed, he rushed back up to his room in the lift, retrieved his swimming trunks and arrived back at the near-deserted leisure complex to sign in. He took the heavenly-soft towel from the woman on the poolside reception and went through into the changing rooms.

After he'd stored his clothes in a locker, he walked down the narrow corridor at the back of the men's changing rooms that opened onto the poolside. The first person he saw was a young woman, or rather a teenage girl. She was immediately visible, reclining on one of the loungers. She was beautiful. Harris realised this the second he saw her and felt a stirring within him – both in his mind and somewhere else – that he hadn't properly felt for anyone before.

He left his towel by a lounger near her and then stepped into the pool. He made sure he did a few lengths before he snuck a look at her again. He was pleasantly surprised to find she was looking at him, too. He smiled. She smiled back. He found he was suddenly desperate to get out of the pool and start talking to her, but he was aware this might make him seem over-eager, perhaps desperate. So he did two more lengths, then climbed out and made a bit of a show of going to a cabinet at the far end housing bottles of Smart Water and took one. As he tipped his head back to drink, he could see she was still looking at him.

'Hey,' she said as he walked up to the lounger and picked up his towel. 'I'm Kelly.'

'Hi,' he said, putting it around his neck and sitting down, hoping he appeared cool, relaxed, attractive, though aware of his heart beating fiercely within him.

There was a pause. It seemed she was waiting for something and it took him some seconds to realise what it was. Then he said, awkwardly, 'Harris. I'm … Harris.'

'You sound like a character in a fairy-tale,' Kelly said, not moving from her lounger, but allowing her eyes to rove over Harris for what felt like a suggestively long time.

'I've only said two words,' Harris said, laughing. Kelly smiled and carried on looking at him.

They sat and talked on the loungers for a while, not noticing the time creep towards 1am. Harris told her he was here with his adopted mum while she did some work. Kelly didn't show a huge interest in this – her uncle was apparently in the movie business and she had come to LA with her brother to stay with him for a bit. He listened as she spoke candidly, and with a flow he found hypnotic, about her childhood in Florida, how she hoped to be an actor and her uncle was going to try to get her roles in a couple of films. 'I feel like I could be like Jennifer Lawrence, or Emma Stone, perhaps, do you know what I mean? Those sorts of roles.' Harris nodded – he would have nodded at anything she said, such was his bewitchment. They talked for another hour until the clock on the wall opposite said 2.15am and Kelly said she should probably get to bed. 'Although I don't have to sleep alone… If you want to join me?' she asked Harris. He stared back at her, stunned and more than a little excited, and felt a prickling sensation on the back of his neck, as though she had whispered the words into his ear. Then, at last, words returned to him.

'Yeah. Yes, I would. Definitely.'

Chapter Twenty-One

HARRIS

Two years before the party

Kelly's room wasn't as large or luxurious as his. She said her uncle had got her and her brother hotel rooms until his apartment was finished being redecorated, then they would go and stay with him in a couple of days' time. Harris had hastily dressed himself in his normal clothes in the changing rooms, but Kelly had brought hers in her bag, choosing to come up in the lift in a soft white hotel bathrobe.

In her room, she slipped off her robe and removed her bikini top with a confidence that made Harris's heart pound. She unbuttoned his shirt and pulled it off him, but as she went to unfasten his jeans she stopped and looked at him. 'You're trembling,' she said, quietly. 'Is it the air conditioning?'

Harris shook his head. 'I'm fine.'

'Come over here,' she said, leading him to the Queen-size bed where she guided him into a sitting position and then pulled off his jeans, casting them aside, before sitting astride his lap and kissing him. The touch of her lips against his felt like a bolt from a heaven he never knew existed, and as her hand travelled down his neck to his chest, she pulled away, her eyes on his. 'Wow, your heart ... you're ... you're really nervous, aren't you?'

Harris nodded. 'Sorry.'

Kelly laughed, but not unkindly. 'Sorry? You don't need to be sorry. Have you ever done this before?'

He paused for a moment, then slowly shook his head.

'You're a virgin?' she asked.

Again he paused, and again he shook his head.

'So...' she said, tilting her gaze for a moment, as if trying to figure him out. 'What are you telling me... I'm sorry, I'm...'

'This is my first time...' he started to say.

She rolled her eyes. 'There's nothing wrong with being a virgin. You're ... what? Sixteen, seventeen?'

'Seventeen. And I'm not a virgin.'

'Right ... so what's going on here?'

'This is my first time ... with a girl ... a woman.'

She stayed still for what felt like an eternity. Then she smiled. 'Ah ... I see.' Then she kissed him again, lightly this time. 'Well, do you want to do it with a girl?'

'Yes,' Harris said, breathlessly, pulling her in closer to him, but he felt her pulling away.

'This isn't some … I don't know … "gay denial" thing is it?' she asked, doing a head tilt again, her eyes a little narrowed.

'What do you mean?'

She got up off his lap and, to his disappointment, settled on the bed next to him, not touching him. 'I mean … you're still going to be gay if we screw or not. It wouldn't change anything.'

'I know,' he said. 'I think I want to … not that I'm in denial or anything… I like girls. Before was just one time and it was … well, it was different.'

Her eyes suddenly go wide. 'Oh, gosh, you weren't, like, attacked or anything?'

Harris hurried to assure her he wasn't.

'Then … I guess there's no problem?'

He nodded slowly. 'I guess.'

Kelly sighed. 'God, I'm sorry, it's … it's your business. I kinda wanted something chilled and easy tonight, but this feels heavy for you and I'm not sure we should … I think the moment's passed.'

Harris was mortified to feel his eyes burning, starting to fill with tears. He mumbled something about needing the bathroom and stumbled towards it. Inside, he washed his face, dabbed at his eyes and, when he was satisfied they didn't look puffy or red, he went back out to Kelly's room. She was watching him closely.

'Come over here,' she said, her voice soft and kind. She pulled up the tightly tucked sheet of the bed and welcomed him under it. He knew as he crawled in they wouldn't be doing anything other than sleeping. And he was fine with that. The tiredness from the long journey and the time difference suddenly caught up with him and within seconds he was asleep in her arms.

He woke suddenly the next morning. He knew at once he'd had a very deep, dreamless sleep, though with this came some confusion. It took him a few moments for it all to come back to him. He was in America. In the hotel. Although this wasn't his room. He could hear the shower running. There were clothes that weren't his on the floor and on a chair near the window.

As he was getting out of bed, the shower stopped abruptly and a few seconds later someone walked out.

Kelly.

'Hi,' she said. She had a towel wrapped around her body and another around her head.

'Er ... hi,' Harris said. He felt awkward. Embarrassed. He wasn't used to situations like this – situations involving waking up in an unknown room with a girl he'd only just met the night before. This was the sort of thing that happened in movies. He suddenly became shy about the fact he was just in his boxer shorts and tried looking round for his trousers but couldn't see them. He figured they were round the other side of the bed. He hadn't been drinking the night before but felt disoriented and confused about how the night had ended. He remembered getting upset, then he and Kelly getting into bed with each other. He couldn't recall the falling asleep part, but he was fairly sure they hadn't had sex. He figured if they had, he wouldn't be wearing his underwear right now. He suddenly felt this was a detail he really needed to know and before he could choose his words carefully, he blurted out 'Did we do it?'

Kelly raised her eyebrows and said 'You're not sure?'

'Oh, shit … that means we did?'

Her eyebrows seemed to rise even further. 'Oh, shit? Interesting choice of words. And for your information, we did not.'

Harris let out a breath.

'That's a relief is it? This isn't quite the 'good morning' of my dreams, Harris,' Kelly said, a little waspishly, going over towards the bed and picking something up. She dropped the items – his jeans and T-shirt down on the bed. 'I didn't get you drunk and seduce you, so I'm not exactly sure why you've got temporary amnesia right now.'

'I haven't… I just got upset and when I get upset I can get confused and … well, I just wanted to be sure about things…'

He saw her expression softening. 'You fell asleep.

Virginity still intact, don't worry. Or woman-virginity, I suppose I should say.'

She began drying herself with a towel. Harris wasn't sure if he should be turning away or if that would annoy her even more. He wasn't even entirely sure if she was annoyed as he thought he could see something close to a smile on her lips. He focused on pulling on his jeans and top and once he was dressed, she'd put on some underwear. God, she was beautiful. He felt a familiar rush of energy in the pit of his stomach and it started to spread through him like an electrical charge, reaching other parts of his anatomy he'd rather not think about at that moment.

'I do, remember, that is,' Harris said. He had a feeling as if he was going backwards, rewinding his past months of cultivating a smooth, calm, cool, well-spoken demeanour and returning to his former awkward self. He half expected to feel his weight returning and his belt tightening, his expensive-label jeans and Ralph Lauren T-shirt returning to a supermarket-brand tracksuit. Of course, this didn't actually occur and after an effort to pull himself together, he found he could talk normally again. 'Thank you for being okay with it, last night. For listening to me and not – well, not making me feel bad.'

She smiled properly then. 'You shouldn't feel bad. Who you do it with for the first time should always be on your terms. Hell, your terms should be pretty fucking important whether it's the first, fifth or five-hundredth time you do it. You should choose the right girl and the right time.'

Harris nodded. 'And I want that to be you.'

Her eyes widened. 'You do?'

Harris nodded. 'Yes. Last night didn't feel right. I was tired and jetlagged and ... well, it just wasn't the right time. But I do want to see you again. I'm here for a week, I think. It might be a bit fluid. My ... Isabelle ... she doesn't tell me much, but I'm pretty sure we'll be here this week, definitely tomorrow. So perhaps we could meet tomorrow night, if you're around?'

Kelly, still smiling, walked over to him. Gently, she kissed him on the lips – just a brief kiss, but it still seemed slow and lingering and afterwards Harris realised he was smiling, too. 'You can take me out to dinner, first,' she said. 'We can go down to one of the restaurants here, then we'll be able to slip upstairs as soon as we're ready.'

Harris agreed. They would meet at 7pm the next evening and swapped numbers so they could WhatsApp if anything changed. They briefly chatted while Kelly got ready for her day, explaining that she and her brother had to do something with their uncle involving a distant relative neither of them liked. Once she was done and apparently satisfied with her hair, she nodded at the door and told him it was time to go. She kissed Harris on the cheek and said goodbye to him in the lift. 'Until tomorrow,' she said.

Harris followed the signs to the restaurant where breakfast was being served. It was an extensive buffet and he helped himself to a large plate of cooked items as well as some cold meats and cheeses, and a bowl of fruit. While he was scanning for a table his eyes fell on Isabelle, who had been watching him from afar. She was seated at a table with three other adults Harris had never seen before. He felt he should go over and at least acknowledge her presence.

'Good morning,' he said as he approached. Everyone at the table had stopped talking and were looking between him and Isabelle.

'Morning, Harris. I hope you've been enjoying yourself.' Isabelle said this in her usual bland, disinterested tone, almost as if she was trotting out a line she felt she should say rather than actually wanted to.

'Yes,' he said, deciding not to share all the details of his adventure the night before.

'This is Harris,' Isabelle explained to her companions. 'I've probably mentioned him before. My husband and I took him in when his parents died just over a year ago.'

Again, this was put in a rather blunt, matter-of-fact way, and Harris felt the achingly familiar pang within him whenever his parents were mentioned.

'Hello, Harris, I'm Susanna,' said one of the others, a blonde woman younger than Isabelle. 'Your hands must be aching holding all that food.' She nodded at Harris's plate and bowl. He wished then he hadn't picked up so much food as he sat at the only empty space.

The man opposite him – also young and extremely good looking – offered his hand and said, 'I'm Craig.' He left it at that.

'And I'm Lucy,' said the other woman in a small, English-accented voice.

'We just needed to finish discussing business,' Isabelle said, taking a sip from her mug of coffee. 'So you can just eat your breakfast while we finish our meeting.'

The idea of a breakfast meeting seemed bizarre to Harris – he usually liked to start the day without speaking to anyone. But they seemed to be in full swing and launched back into the discussion they'd been having before Harris had sat down.

'I know availability might be tight, but I really think he'd be perfect for the role,' Craig said, his voice loud and strong.

'I'm yet to be convinced,' said Isabelle.

'Me, too,' said Susanna.

'What's he been in again?' asked Lucy.

'There's just something a bit *toxic* about him,' said Susanna, ignoring her.

'Toxic how?' asked Isabelle.

'In a toxic-masculinity sort of way,' explained Susanna.

'Really?' said Isabelle.

'How?' asked Craig.

'He gave Greta Gerwig's last two movies one star on Letterboxd,' said Susanna.

'Oh, shit,' said Craig.

'Exactly,' said Susanna.

'What's Letterboxd?' asked Lucy.

'He's also been a bit outspoken about the current climate,' went on Susanna.

'Climate as in climate *change*?' said Craig, 'oh, fuck.'

'No, not climate *change*, although we'll come back to that, I meant the current climate as in, you know, cancel culture et cetera…' Susanna sighed. 'He thinks things have gone too far.'

'Of course things have gone too fucking far,' said Craig, 'but rule number one is that you don't fucking say they've gone too fucking far, otherwise you find out how fucking far things really can fucking go.'

'I don't understand, what's he actually said?' asked Lucy.

'Well, we'll strike him off the list,' said Craig, 'you've talked me out of it, Susanna.' He magicked up a large iPad seemingly out of nowhere and began to jab at it. Harris ate a piece of pineapple, rather transfixed by the entire exchange.

'I'll sound out Natasha about it,' Isabelle said. 'I'm going to see her today. She looked at her watch. 'In fact, I should get moving.' She got up. Harris, who was just moving on to his main plate of food looked up at her. She stayed standing there, her eyebrows raised, looking expectantly at him. He got the message and rose, too.

'The poor guy's hardly finished his breakfast,' Susanna said, doing a mock look of pity at Harris.

'Yes, well, we can get something on the way if needed,' Isabelle said. There was a tight look on her face that Harris recognised as her stressed-about-something look. He wondered what it was. Perhaps today's visit to Natasha was going to be a fraught affair.

As they walked through the corridor out to the main reception, Isabelle turned to look at Harris and said, 'Christ, your top's all creased. And...' She leaned forward and sniffed his hair. 'You smell of chorine. Have you been in the pool?'

'Er ... yes,' he said. 'I was going to head back there now if that's okay?'

Her eyes flashed. 'Of course it's not okay, I told you, we're expected at Natasha's. This is a very important meeting, Harris.'

He frowned, thrown by this. 'I hope it goes well, but ... what does that have to do with me?'

'You're coming with me, I'm sure I told you about this,' she said, rummaging in her bag for her phone.

'You didn't,' Harris said.

'Well, you know now. Come on, we'll find you something to wear. You'll have to have the fastest shower of your life while I iron something.'

Iron something. He'd never heard such strange words

come out of Isabelle's mouth – indeed, he'd never seen her holding anything as homely or domestic as an iron. All that was usually left to Emmeline.

Up in his room, Harris took a shower – he'd been practically thrown into the en suite of his hotel bedroom – whilst Isabelle wrestled a shirt out of his bag and proceeded to attack it with silent intensity using an iron she'd found bagged up in the cupboard. She'd also laid out jeans and socks for him, each item waiting for him on the bed. He found this weird and was tempted to ask what was going on, but her steely gaze made him think otherwise. She went over to the window while he dressed, although seemed to be more preoccupied with her phone than the view.

'Ready,' he said once he'd pulled on his shoes.

'At last.' Isabelle walked past him and opened the door to the corridor outside. 'Come on.'

They were driven in a black Mercedes with tinted windows and aggressive air conditioning. Isabelle continued to tap on her phone throughout the journey. Eventually, Harris could hold back his curiosity no longer.

'I don't understand why I have to—'

'Natasha showed an interest in you when you met her in London,' Isabelle said in a clipped voice, pre-empting his question.

'I've met her?'

She sighed. 'Of course you've met her. At Claridge's.'

Harris was confused for a moment. Then he remembered the odd meeting with the handsome, but rather intimidating American lady that day he'd needed a lift back from London.

'Oh, her,' he said.

'Yes, her.'

'And she wants … to see me again? Me?'

Another sigh from Isabelle. 'She suggested the meeting would go better if you were there. I think she likes to … um … dote on people. Likes to have an audience. You are that audience. Just sit there, look pretty, smile at whatever she says to you and hopefully we'll have her signed up and on board by the end of the afternoon.'

Harris frowned. 'You want me to help you sign her up for a role in your movie?'

He saw Isabelle roll her eyes. 'It isn't *my* movie. I'm hired by the production company. But yes, in a nutshell.'

Harris didn't ask any more questions for the rest of the journey. He just watched out of the darkened glass as the main road turned into a winding maze of pavement-less streets, crawling past mansions of various designs, a lot of them crammed together, separated by gates and stone walls. At one of these, the car turned and began up an incline driveway, passing through gates which opened without any apparent intervention.

'Get out, we're here,' Isabelle instructed.

Harris opened the door and was immediately hit by

the warm air and sunshine. Blinking, he pulled his shades out of his pocket. The house was a mixture of neo-English country-manor and ultra-modern, with wings that looked like extensions, and an overall 'fake' feel to the whole thing. A young man walked out of the dark-wood front doors and over to the car.

'Good afternoon, you must be Ms Moncrieff,' the man said, offering a hand. He had an athletic build, short hair and was dressed in white trousers and a dark blue polo shirt. 'I'm Armando, Natasha's personal assistant.'

'Of course you are,' Isabelle said, looking him up and down, and Harris thought he could see her lip curl, almost like she disapproved of this polite, good-looking young man.

'And this must be your son,' he said, offering the same hand to Harris, who shook it. Before he could say anything, Isabelle said, 'No, not really, Harris just lives with us. Shall we go through and find Natasha?'

'Right this way.'

They were led through the entrance hall and through an expansive living room area with a high ceiling and exposed beams. Natasha was seated outside at a table underneath an impressive-sized umbrella. Two separate swimming pools stretched off into the distance, connected by a bridge in between, the larger of the two branching off into a canal that led away through the trees at the far end. Harris couldn't help but think how much fun he would have had if he'd been able to play in such an area when he was a child.

'Oh, yes, it's you, Isabelle,' Natasha sniffed, looking up from a doorstopper hardback novel with an ornate gold-embossed cover. 'Are you here to rescue me from this turgid volume of debauchery.' She cast the book aside. 'I do wonder why writers find it so hard to write sex and violence these days. It's so difficult to know how much blood to ladle on when it's not an outright horror. I might just wait for the screenplay to be written. Then I'll have a better idea.' She yawned widely, raising the back of her hand to her mouth. Then she caught sight of Harris and froze. Rising from her seat she came over to them.

'Oh, yes ... you're here too. She *actually* brought you.' Her eyes flicked from him to Isabelle. 'Interesting.' If she'd seemed tired and disinterested seconds before, she was now very much alert, all smiles and kindness, welcoming them over to another seated area round the side of the house in the shade with sofas and a large table. 'Armando,' she called. The man appeared. 'Bring ... some ... pastries! Yes, we must have pastries and...' She paused, looking at Isabelle and Harris, as if hoping they'd chime in with suggestions, and when neither of them did, she clapped her hands and said, 'I know, strawberry lemonade. Yes, lemonade! In fact, a variety of lemonades! Maybe some ... um ... something nice, something a bit stronger, to put in mine.'

Armando nodded diligently and disappeared off. Pastries and lemonade did indeed appear a few moments later and they politely nibbled at the buttery croissants and tarts, Harris all the while finding his presence there strange and puzzling. Things got stranger still when Isabelle set down her pastry suddenly and said 'Oh, God. I'm so sorry, I completely forgot, I've got another appointment on the other side of town. It won't take long, though.' She made a show of looking at her phone. 'I could be back within two hours and we can continue discussing the film then. And to pick up Harris, of course. You'll be okay here while I pop out for an hour or two, won't you?'

Harris stared at her, and then at Natasha. They hadn't even begun discussing the film, so that didn't make any sense to him, neither did being left there alone with this woman he didn't know. But Isabelle didn't wait for a reply, she just left.

'Don't worry about her,' Natasha said, sliding onto the sofa next to Harris. 'We can have a chat. And get to know each other.'

But Harris did worry – he was disconcerted and confused and got up, walking away from the outside dining area and around the house and back the way they'd come. He caught up with Isabelle just as she was getting into the car on the driveway.

'Wait! Why are you—'

'For God's sake, Harris, go back outside. Just stay here and ... do what she asks.'

'What?' he said, baffled.

'Use your imagination, Harris,' she said, coming over to him. 'I think you know what she's after. Just ... you're a teenage boy. She's a glamorous actress. Most lads your age would pay good money for this opportunity.'

Harris opened his mouth, closed it again, then realised he had no words to reply.

'I'll put it bluntly. You're a good-looking young man. She's into that. So just turn on your charm and earn your fucking keep, okay?'

Harris didn't have the chance to say whether it was okay or not. Isabelle opened the car door, got in and drove off.

Chapter Twenty-Two

HARRIS

Two years before the party

Harris stood in bewilderment, wondering what had just happened. As he tried to make sense of Isabelle's words, he felt someone behind him. He jumped and turned around to find Armando standing there.

'Would you like to come back into the garden?' he said, putting an arm on Harris's shoulder. 'Ms Crewe has suggested a swim and has suggested you can change in the pool house. I'll show you where it is.'

Harris followed Armando back out to the poolside in a daze. They crossed the bridge separating the two pools and he saw that the smaller one had jets under the water and must be more of an oversized jacuzzi built into the ground. They walked towards the expanse of trees, though still staying around the pool edge, until they came to what looked like a summer house, although Harris thought it looked bigger than many actual houses.

'I ... don't have any swim shorts with me,' Harris said.

'You'll find everything you need waiting for you inside.' Armando said. 'And don't worry. She won't bite. I can promise you that. Not unless you ask her to.' He winked at Harris, then turned to walk back towards the house.

Harris opened the door. The interior was just one room, consisting of a small table and white wooden chairs, upon which were piles of soft-looking towels and a lamp. In the middle of the room was a bed. Harris froze. On the bed, was a woman. Natasha. She was naked, lying on her back, one arm behind her head, the other resting by her side. Her legs were apart.

'Here's my handsome boy,' she cooed, and chuckled a little.

Harris felt as if he was walking through a dream. His senses felt dulled, muted, as if what was happening wasn't real. He found it was easy to do as Natasha asked – to remove his top and take off his trousers, all while she watched on. He stood there as naked as she was, and when she raised her arm and held her hand out towards him, he did the only thing he could think of. He took it.

Harris was swimming lengths in the pool when Isabelle returned. It was hard to read her expression because she had sunglasses on, though he saw her glance at him as she walked around to the table where they'd all sat just a couple of hours before. She proceeded to pull out a black folder and set it open on the table. Natasha was already sitting there – she'd been watching Harris swim, a lazy smile on her face. They said something to each other, but Harris couldn't quite hear it through the sound of the water lapping around him. He swam to the side and pulled himself out, just as Natasha closed the folder and said, 'God, when I see printed documents like that I regret firing my useless agent. Never mind. I'm pleased it's all settled.'

'This isn't the contract, it's a bible-doc for the whole project so you have a complete view of casting and script changes. It's so good to have you on board. I'll have the contract emailed over,' Isabelle said. Then she turned to Harris. 'Go and get dressed. We'll be leaving in a few minutes.'

As he pulled on his clothes in the pool house, Harris looked at the bed. It was no longer made, the sheet a mixture of creases and folds.

He thought back to an hour ago, when he was on top of Natasha, holding onto her shoulders, pushing into her, her arms and legs wrapped around him. Or when she'd asked him to do other things. Other positions. Other actions. Ones that made her gasp and call out in pleasure and him grunt and groan. He couldn't believe how easily he'd done it. How strangely vacant his mind had been. Had he wanted to? He must have done. He'd be lying if he said he hadn't got a thrill from it, felt the pleasure as he moved inside her. But it felt as if that had been another person who had done that. Separated from the here and now.

And then, as he closed the door to the summer house and went back along the poolside to the house, his thoughts went to Kelly. To the conversation they'd had this morning and the plans they'd made for that very evening. An evening he now knew wouldn't happen. He wasn't sure why he couldn't face her, but he knew it was an impossibility. The moment had gone. Taken from him. Stolen from him. By Natasha Crewe. And, in a way, by Isabelle, too.

Without quite knowing why, something broke inside of him then. A piece of him he never knew he had, a fracture in his mind – a ripple of regret and resentment, anger and pain. And he just wanted to get away from this place. He just wanted to escape. Most of all, he wanted his mum. But he knew that wasn't possible. So he stayed silent as he went up to Isabelle and then followed her out to the car. He didn't reply to Natasha when she called out goodbye to him. He just got into the car, did up his belt and faced forward, trying to ignore the pricking sensation in his eyes.

As the car turned out onto the road, he felt his phone

buzz in his pocket. It was a message. From Kelly. *'Quick swim before dinner? See you at the pool at 6pm?'*

Harris paused for a moment, his hand hovering over the phone. Then he deleted the message from his WhatsApp along with Kelly's contact details.

'Thank you,' Isabelle said during the journey back. She briefly turned to look at Harris and when he didn't respond she didn't say anything else. It would be the only time she'd ever reference what happened on that trip to California.

At least, it was the only time until a few years later, when her son's engagement party was in full swing.

Chapter Twenty-Three

HARRIS

The day of the party

O nce she has got Harris away from Elena and Pippa, Isabelle stares at him with a look of horror in her face. Then she gains control of herself. Purses her lip. Surveys him with something close to hatred.

'Don't you dare,' she says, her voice quiet and dangerous.

'I'm sorry?' Harris says, smiling pleasantly at her.

'Don't even think about it.'

'Think about what?' asks Harris, continuing to keep his expression relaxed, innocent, vaguely interested.

'You know what I'm talking about,' she says.

'I think that's my line,' says Harris, now allowing his smile to twist into a half-smirk, which seemed to enrage Isabelle even further.

'I think you've had too much to drink.'

'I don't think so,' said Harris, placidly. 'I'm just starting to remember a lot of details all of a sudden. You never know, maybe the alcohol has jogged my memory. It can, I suppose. Open doors that were once shut, filled with those interesting details. They mount up, you know. Details. Sometimes they just … topple over with no warning.' He takes a step forward. 'It's hard to keep conversation under control when there's so much to talk about. So much.'

He sees fear in her eyes, coupled with the anger. 'I … you … you're *enjoying* this, aren't you. Playing with me. Well, it's not going to work, Harris. I don't know what you think … what you think happened…'

'What? The day you whored out your seventeen-year-old adopted son to a neurotic drug-addicted film star more than twice his age.'

'Don't give me that—' Isabelle starts to say, casting a frightened glance around the guests walking along the terrace nearby.

'Did you know that she drugged *me*?' Harris says, still keeping his tone light. 'Oh, yes. I found out everything. At a film premiere we all went to some months later, I bumped into that housekeeper-toyboy of hers, Armando. I avoided her, Natasha that is, but he sought me out at the after-party and told me about the pills. Said he thought I ought to know as he wasn't happy about it. Apparently, he didn't realise she'd slipped me something until he found the packets and she tried to joke with him afterwards. Something was in the drinks she got us – strawberry lemonade, I think it was. My glass had a covert special ingredient. It was Diazepam or Oxycodone – Armando says it could have been either since she uses both a lot. Unlikely I had both together, otherwise I would have been sleeping on that pool house bed of hers, rather than blearily letting her seduce me. I was still able to fuck her, to be fair. I wasn't passing out at any point. But it's all a bit *dodgy*, isn't it? Especially when drugs are involved. That aspect truly is the icing on the sick little cake, isn't it?'

Isabelle seems to sway ever so slightly on the spot. 'I never … never knew…'

'Oh, well that's fine, then,' Harris says, beaming at her. 'Anyway, I shouldn't keep you. I should keep mingling. Put on that handsome-boy charm you particularly approve of, start talking to *your* guests.' He says the final words with relish, suggesting he has a lot to tell them. He gives her a short nod as a form of goodbye and walks away from her.

As he moves round the side entrance of the grand house, he notices Rhys sidle up to him. He'd almost forgotten he was here, his mind had been so focused on his family. 'What did you say to her?'

Harris rolls his eyes. 'Don't worry. I didn't give the game away. I just…' he sighed.

'Just what?' Rhys asks, urgently. 'Listen, if you're having second thoughts, we could just…'

'No. I'm not having second thoughts. I wanted to ruffle her feathers a little. Can't have her enjoying the day too much.'

'Okay, well, just don't ruffle those feathers too thoroughly. Or you'll give the game away.'

'Very true,' Harris says, 'we don't want to lessen the shock later. We want impact on our side when it's time.'

He allows a few moments of silence pass while his mind flits to the future. After everything's finished. When the bridges are so burned there'll be no way back. Finally, he asks, 'Is it done?'

Rhys nods. 'I think so. Everything should be done. Providing nobody notices anything's wrong beforehand, it should all work exactly how we planned. Although you'll have to act quickly. There's every chance they'll try to stop you when they suss what you're doing. As I said, I'm not sure you'll have enough time.'

Harris taps him on the arm. 'Don't worry about that,' he says. 'I'll have enough time. Enough to do the damage they deserve.'

Part III

_____

THE CRIMES OF PATRICK MONCRIEFF

Chapter Twenty-Four

PATRICK

Twenty-one years before the party

On the day Patrick Moncrieff first met the woman who would become Harris's mother, his property-investment company, Excellere, had recently moved to its gleaming new headquarters in Battersea. A celebration was being held in the offices – mostly in the lobby, but people were filtering up to the other floors the business occupied. Some people were still working, hurriedly getting things checked off their to-do list before accepting a glass of champagne. One of these people was Erin Strong, who was still sat at her desk forty-five minutes into the party.

'My God, you're dedicated,' Patrick said, setting down his glass on the desk surface as he leaned in to look at Erin's screen. 'What could possibly be so important for you to miss champagne and a range of gourmet pizzas?'

Erin looked up, surprise in her eyes at first, but then laughed. 'Oh, I was just checking numbers for a batch of brochures going to the printers.'

Patrick nodded, raising his eyebrows to show he was impressed. 'Well, you're clearly an asset to the team.' He held out a hand. 'I'm Patrick Moncrieff, I'm—'

'The boss, yes, I know,' said Erin. She didn't seem to be nervous about talking to 'the boss' or particularly deferential. He quite liked that. He got bored with the staff members who treated him like royalty or were overly sycophantic, enthusiastically agreeing with things he suspected they disagreed with just to keep in his good graces.

'I need to do a good job,' Erin said, simply. 'You probably don't know, but I'm a temp. Both me and Laila, who sits next to me,' she motioned with a hand to the empty desk beside her. 'We're both supplied by an agency. And I need a good reference, otherwise I may not get another position after this one.'

Patrick frowned. 'Who is your line manager? Belinda?' He glanced down the end of the office to where Belinda was glugging down champagne – not her first or her second, he suspected. 'Ah, a positive write-up from Belinda is a tall order. Perhaps you should approach her when she's drunk, she'll likely be far more reasonable.'

Erin smiled but there was something severe in her eyes. 'You shouldn't talk about my superior like that to me. It isn't professional.'

Patrick found himself grinning back even wider. Being told off by one of his employees – especially one as beautiful and charismatic as Erin – was a new sensation and he was rather enjoying it. 'Perhaps I feel I can be candid with you.'

She held his gaze. 'I see.'

The two words hung between them for a moment, as if they were weighted with a subtext neither of them dared acknowledge. Then the spell was broken by what she said next.

'I'll come down and have a drink now, but I won't be able to stay long. My husband and I live in Ilford and it's a rather long commute.'

Patrick felt the disappointment starting to spread through him. He had secretly been hoping they were destined for the store cupboard with her on her knees in front of him while he struggled to keep his moans quiet. But it seemed this was to remain a hopeful fantasy – at least for tonight.

'I could give you a lift home?' he asked. One last attempt to turn the night around. The possibility of a secluded street. A reclining seat. Tinted windows.

'No, it's fine,' she said, getting up. 'It was nice to meet you in person, though.' Then she walked away from him towards Belinda and the group she was talking to, as Patrick watched her go with close attentiveness.

The affair started a month later. After a few weeks of avoiding each other, helped by Patrick's frequent travelling, they eventually both found themselves alone in the office again one unseasonably chilly April evening after Erin, who had left the office a couple of hours earlier, had come back to get her scarf.

'You came all the way from Ilford to get a scarf?' Patrick asked, walking past the empty desks, trying to keep his pace slow, casual, unhurried, in control.

'No, I was having dinner with friends over in Vauxhall, so I wasn't far away.'

Patrick nodded. He liked the way she was looking at him. Eyes bright, steady, comfortable holding his. The cold temperatures outside had caused a slight flush to her usually pale cheeks. He liked it. Felt it made her even more beautiful.

'I don't have long,' she said.

'That's okay,' he replied, quietly.

'I mean here. At your company. My contract ends in fifteen days. Working days, that is.'

'Well, then,' he said, coming to a stop now directly in front of her. 'We'd better make up for lost time.'

'You okay?' he asked, quietly.

She sighed. 'Yeah. I think I am. It's just … well, I can't help but think that it's a bit sad. You're so hugely successful for someone so young. A handsome, wealthy aristocrat who doesn't sit around wasting his life—'

'I'm not sure I think of myself as an aristocrat,' he cut in. 'Old money doesn't have to mean aristocratic.'

She shrugged. 'Regardless, few men in their twenties have such power in business and a wife and a beautiful house. But you've chosen to do this with me. I don't know whether to be flattered and leave it at that, or feel bad that you feel you need to.'

He frowned at her. 'How do you know about my wife and how supposedly beautiful my house is?'

Even in the darkness, he could make out the roll of her eyes. 'If you want to keep any privacy, perhaps don't agree to journalists doing features on you in lifestyle magazines. "Young, hot, property magnet" was I think how they referred to you.'

That had made him smile. 'I just acquire land and buildings. Put up more buildings, *better* buildings, pocket the profit. Use it to go it again. It's not rocket science.'

'You see, it's interesting you qualified that part,' she said, 'and not the young and hot part.'

'Well, regardless, you don't need to be sad for me. I'm doing just fine.' He leant forwards and put his hand on the back of her neck. 'Are you going to tell your husband about this?'

'No,' she said. There was a quiet certainty in her voice he admired.

'Are we going to do this again?'

'Yes,' she said. Then she leant forward to kiss him. Her making the move this time. But it was an equal kiss, one they both entered into. A kiss of energy, thrill, an electric buzz conjured out of the evening's actions.

When they stopped and looked at each other, Patrick said, 'Do you know what the best thing is about having money?'

She didn't answer, just stared back at him.

'It's being able to have it all. People say you can't, but you really fucking can.'

He hoped the words would impress her, but she just reached for her bag in the footwell and said 'Well, that's … good for you.'

'I mean this is all going to work out very well for both of us,' Patrick said. 'I mean it. Just you wait. This is going to work out exactly how I want it to. Things always do.'

Erin gave him an odd look – confusion mixed with something else that he couldn't place. Then she got out of the car and walked towards her home. He watched her go in, then drove away, back to his city apartment. Perhaps he'd phone Isabelle, tell her he'd be back home at the weekend, but not tomorrow. Tomorrow he'd be busy putting a few things in place. Getting things sorted. He had a contact who was in the process of opening a new gallery space in Whitechapel. He'd speak to him, see if he was potentially hiring. Then he would look at what available empty properties he had. Yes, he would be very busy tomorrow. Making sure life continued to go his way.

Chapter Twenty-Five

PATRICK

Nineteen years before the party

Patrick and Isabelle arrived in Ecclestone Square late for the dinner party they were attending. They had been staying at a hotel in Chesham Place for a few days, with Isabelle taking the time to catch up with some studio contacts in Soho, a short taxi ride away, while Patrick had been looking around several office-space investments in Mayfair and Marble Arch. Isabelle had suggested taking a cab to the dinner party, then returning to the hotel to collect their car, but Patrick had wanted to drive so they could make a quick getaway afterwards. 'Do what you want,' sighed Isabelle. She hadn't really wanted to go. To her, Erin and John were a couple they'd met at a gallery opening. Patrick had mentioned dismissively that Erin had briefly worked for his company before moving into the art world, but didn't go into details. Didn't mention that he was the one who had helped get her the job and made it possible for her to move with John to central London. He was aware the couple weren't of the class of people Isabelle would normally like to connect with. So when she did agree to a meet-up, she was usually irritable and distant. He wondered sometimes how much she knew, how much she guessed and how much she chose to turn a blind eye to. He dared not ask, just in case the whole thing started to unravel. So they just carried on. Patrick was quite proud of how well he'd managed the whole situation. Sometimes he hardly believed he'd got away with it.

'Erin said there'd be a parking space free near the gate to the gardens.' He nodded towards a padlocked metal gate visible in the gloom across the road.

'Well she was obviously wrong,' Isabelle said. 'Maybe some of the other guests have taken it.'

'There's only the Medlows,' Patrick said, driving further away from their destination and down a neighbouring street. 'They normally walk over from Elizabeth Street.' They eventually found a space and walked back to the square, Isabelle lagging behind, something Patrick hated and recognised as her way of showing her lack of enthusiasm about the whole evening.

Erin and John welcomed them at the doorstep. 'Heya, great to see you both,' Erin said. Patrick noticed Isabelle wince at the *"Heya"*. These were the sorts of people Isabelle would prefer not to associate with. She was a snob through and through and the trace of Essex vowels in Erin's accent would be enough to put Isabelle's teeth on edge. He disliked this side to his wife, though at times couldn't help finding it a little amusing.

'Sorry we're late,' Isabelle said without enthusiasm, removing her coat. 'Parking was a bit of a difficulty.' Dig number one, Patrick thought to himself.

'Oh, sorry,' John said. 'That will be Charlie's car. He's moved into the basement.'

This made Patrick freeze. 'Sorry, *what*? Who's moved into the basement?' His reaction caused the hosts and his wife to turn to look at him.

'We've got a lodger,' John said. 'A nice man. A lad, really, very young, posh old family, but not in an uppity way. He wanted to get out from under his parents' feet, I think. They have a house on St George's Square. Very close. But it's good for a young man to have his own space.'

He couldn't quite believe what he was hearing. 'Sorry, I'm confused. Who's he renting from? How ... I don't.'

'Patrick, what's wrong with you?' Isabelle said, letting out an exasperated breath. 'They've just explained, they've got a lodger. In their basement. Is it really that hard to understand?'

He'd heard all that. Each word had registered in some way, just not in a way he could sort into an order that made sense. He just couldn't believe the audacity of it. The underhand way it had happened. He looked at Erin. She was avoiding eye contact with him. He needed to pull it together. His surprise and anger had already made things awkward. The last thing he needed was Isabelle asking suspicious questions all the way home.

'Sorry. Of course. Well, I'm sure we'd … um … be fascinated to meet this … um … lodger.'

'Oh he's not here today,' John said. 'Visiting a friend in Chelsea, I think he said.'

He was aware Isabelle was still looking at him as if he'd gone completely mad. Perhaps he had, he thought, as they were ushered into the kitchen-dining area where the Medlows were already seated. Patrick knew Isabelle would have thought it common to be shown straight to where they were dining, rather than be given drinks in another room first, but to be fair, he reasoned, they were quite late and perhaps Erin and John thought it best to move things along.

They settled into their places while John poured the wine. Erin put her hand over her glass when he got to her. 'Oh, yes, I forgot, sorry love,' he said and moved on. Patrick didn't miss this. He fixed his gaze intently on Erin until eventually she said, 'I've had a bit of vertigo, recently. Labyrinthitis, perhaps. Effects the balance. Doctor said I had to lay off the alcohol for a while. Make sure I'm staying steady and all that.'

Patrick gave a raise of the chin, as if to say 'I see,' then took a sip of his own wine.

After dinner, there was a moment when Patrick spotted Erin had left the table, presumably to use the bathroom. He made his excuse to do the same and cornered her on the stairs as she was coming down.

'We need to talk,' he muttered, quietly. He took her by the hand around the corner of the banisters and down the steps that led to the basement of the property.

'We can't go down here, this is Charlie's flat now,' she said.

'Is it locked?' he asked, then tried the door. 'Splendid.'

'Patrick, no... It's a betrayal of trust,' she said, sounding stressed as she followed him through into the flat. He turned the light on and looked around. There were boxes still yet to be unpacked. Towels slung onto the bed. Haphazard piles of underwear and clothing waiting to be sorted. Two towering stacks of well-read Penguin Classics on the floor. A desk with a rather new-looking laptop on its surface.

'Ironic that you say a betrayal of trust,' Patrick muttered.

'I know we should have told you,' Erin said.

'No, you shouldn't have told me. You should have *asked* me. Since I'm the owner, renting out this place without—'

'Oh come on, Patrick, stop being so dramatic.'

He surveyed her. 'What does John think?'

She sighed. Bit her lip. But didn't answer.

'What if he found out that this place isn't actually owned by your Great Aunt Elda in Scotland?' He took a step towards her. Brought himself close. 'What if he realised that the house and the rental agency you pay a pittance to are in fact both owned –' he purposefully let his breath gush against her neck '– by me.' He felt her respond. Pulled her in close. 'What if he found out what you like to do...' He moved his hand downwards, 'when he's not around?'

Without warning, he pushed her down onto Charlie's bed. She fell amidst the towels and discarded clothes. 'This is dangerous, your *wife* is upstairs,' she hissed, but he could feel that she wanted it, and didn't protest as he moved his hand up her skirt.

'I like that it's dangerous,' he said breathlessly, unbuckling his belt. He tugged down his trousers, gasped and grunted, feeling a rush of light-headedness. He moved, tilted forwards, deep and strong, feeling her hands on his back, holding him tight.

'Are you cross with me?' she whispered in his ear.

'Very,' he said, allowing his moans and groans to continue to escape him while at the same time hoping their sounds wouldn't carry up the stairs.

'Are you going to punish me?' she asked, her voice shaking.

'Yes,' he said, his hand going to her neck, pushing

more forcefully into her. 'I'm going to fuck you any time I want and any way I want.' He drove inside her even harder, feeling her start to tense. 'And I'm going to remind you that this London life you're enjoying – it's all because of me.' He tightened his grip on her neck, pulling back to look at her. His eyes narrowed as they fixed on hers. 'And you're going to do as you're told, or your husband – ' he flipped her over and re-entered her, quickly and roughly, making her gasp '– is going to find out you're not the rich catch he thinks you are.'

He started to build the momentum, but she reached around, putting a hand on his arm, her grip strong. He was forgetting where he was, enjoying how everything about this situation was setting his brain on fire – an electric, wildly compelling fire he welcomed and embraced.

'Just don't punish me too roughly,' she said, her voice sounding more normal all of a sudden.

'Why not?' he said, continuing his movements. 'Why should I go easy on you. I think … I think you deserve to feel the full force of my displeasure. Because you've displeased me, Erin. And people who displease me need to know that their transgressions will be punished. So why should I go easy on you? Why are *you* so special?'

A beat of silence passed when all he could hear were his own quickening breaths. Then she spoke.

'Because I'm pregnant.'

The world stopped. Patrick couldn't move. They

stayed where they were motionless for what felt like an age. Then he pulled away from her. 'But ... you can't be.'

'Well, I am,' she said, turning round, pulling up her underwear and straightening her dress. 'And it's yours. I ... I have been meaning to tell you.'

He stared at her. '*Meaning* to tell me?' He could still hear his heart, but now it was beating fast for an entirely different reason. And he didn't like the sound of it at all. 'Meaning to tell me?' he repeated, breathlessly. 'The same way you've been meaning to tell me about the lodger in this flat? Is ... is there anything else?'

She shook her head.

'Fuck,' he said, putting his hand to his head. Then he pulled up his trousers, did up his belt, and fixed his gaze up on her once more. 'Get rid of it,' he said.

'No,' she replied, simply. She sat there, on the edge of the bed, matching his stare.

'If you don't—'

'Don't threaten me again, Patrick. This suited you when it did, but now it's looking a bit too messy, isn't it?' She pulled herself up. 'Well, I'm not going to be cast aside. You're going to carry on letting me live here, carry on paying the bills, and I won't tell John anything. I won't tell your wife anything. And I won't tell little Raphael anything.'

His mind flitted back to his house in Bath. His baby boy, being cared for by their put-upon young housekeeper Emmeline.

'Don't be sick,' he said. 'He's ... he's a child.'

'For now,' Erin said, 'but when he's older, he may want to know he has a sibling. I also doubt your wife would like the whole situation. Although I dare say she's more clued up on things than you think she is.'

He felt a flash of something within him. A white cold anger. He stepped forward, raising his fist.

He didn't know what would have happened if his wife's voice hadn't travelled down the stairs at that point. He didn't know if he would have lowered his clenched hand, put it down to a sudden moment of madness. Or if he would have done something worse. But the voice caused him to freeze, disrupting the moment.

That didn't stop him seeing the look in Erin's eyes.

'I always knew you were that sort of man, deep down,' she said, looking at his fist.

He didn't know what to say. So he walked out of the basement, back up the stairs.

'Patrick, you've been ages,' Isabelle said as he came back into the kitchen. 'We need to get going.'

'Yes, we do,' he said, suddenly feeling short of breath. He tried to steady himself, desperate for nobody else to spot the mental turmoil that was enveloping him. 'Yes. We should leave. It's time to go home.'

Chapter Twenty-Six

HARRIS

One year before the party

Harris often found the extended periods at home during the school holidays a bit of a trial. If Patrick was there, he found him too attentive, always trying to get him to play golf at one of the local clubs, or embrace a boozy lunch at a nearby hotel or in one of the private members clubs in Bath. Often, though, Patrick was away on business, which was fine where Harris was concerned, although it meant he had to endure Isabelle on her own.

On this occasion, both Patrick and Isabelle were around for the Easter break, and Patrick convinced Harris that they should go for a meal to celebrate his eighteenth birthday. 'Or we could throw a party,' he said. 'Ask your friends over. They could stay if you wanted?'

Harris declined. He'd find the whole thing awkward and he liked keeping his home life relatively separate. So the meal out felt like a good compromise, although the dinner became more about Raphael's new girlfriend Lauren. His parents were welcoming and friendly towards her (albeit in a guarded, distant way on Isabelle's part) although Harris noted her share a concerned glance with Patrick when it was revealed Lauren was nearly ten years older than their son and had been his seminar tutor – a role she'd taken on as part of her PhD.

'And is ... the university okay with that?' Isabelle asked, a frown creasing her brow.

'Well, we haven't exactly told them,' Lauren said, beaming, looking over at Raphael. 'But my Raphy is just so irresistible, I'm sure nobody would mind if they found out.'

Harris almost choked on his Coke when he heard the term 'Raphy' but managed to stifle his laughter.

'Well, an age difference is no bad thing,' Patrick said, trying to sound calm and casual.

Harris watched as the topic of his birthday meal became almost exclusively about Lauren and her upbringing, her highly Christian parents and grandparents. She had a way of speaking that reminded Harris a little of a character from a period drama ('My father is a generally very agreeable man and we write often – a joyfully unhurried form of communication, would you not agree, Raphy?') It came as no surprise to anybody that Lauren's PhD was in Georgian Literature.

Raphael drove her home afterwards and Harris went back in the car with Patrick and Isabelle. As they entered the hallway, Isabelle remarked that there was some post set aside for Harris. Feeling tired and not really paying attention, he picked up the small pile.

There was a magazine from a subscription Harris had lost interest in, a loyalty card offer for a retailer, and an envelope made of such high-quality cream paper that his interest was immediately piqued. On the back, the return address sounded familiar. Then he realised where he'd heard the business's name before.

'Something interesting?' Patrick asked, hanging up his coat.

'No,' Harris said, more bluntly and loudly than he meant to. He saw Patrick raise his eyes in surprise. 'Er ... just rubbish.'

Harris hurried upstairs to his bedroom, sat down on his bed and opened the envelope. Inside was a letter from the firm of lawyers who had overseen the legal aspects of his parents' deaths and Harris's inheritance. The lawyer, named Jason Booth, was requesting a meeting with Harris in London and asked him to give his secretary a call or email. He remembered Mr Booth from the discussions to do with inheritance and his adoption that had occurred when his parents had died. He didn't give much away in the letter, but implied the meeting had a connection with Harris now becoming an adult and a final bequest left to him by one or both of his parents.

'What's that?' a voice called from the door.

He looked up to see Raphael standing there, leaning against the doorframe.

'I thought you were taking Lauren home?' Harris said, confused.

'I did. But to the train station, not all the way. Didn't want to drive her all the way to her parents' house. She's staying with them at the moment and they... Well, as you heard, they don't quite know about us yet.'

Harris nodded, his mind on the letter in his hand. He saw on the clock on the bedside table that nearly a whole hour had passed since he'd opened it, time had been swallowed up by thoughts and the memories of his mum, his dad, his life in London. It was as if a dream he'd almost forgotten had rushed back to the surface of his mind.

'So,' said Raphael, nodding over at the letter. 'What is it?'

'Nothing,' Harris said, pushing it aside.

Raphael walked further in and before Harris could stop him picked it up.

'Strange,' he said, reading it through. 'Do you know what it could be about? Maybe you've got more money coming to you. Though I would have thought Dad would have told you if that was happening.'

Harris shrugged. He didn't want to discuss this with Raphael. Although over the years, they'd edged towards something closer to friends, Harris had never felt like Raphael was someone he could confide in – or want to confide in. He thought he knew Raphael's motivations. How he was awkward with what had transpired between them. In his own repressed sort of way perhaps he wanted to make amends. Harris wasn't ready to forgive. But he also wasn't keen on conflict.

'I'm going to London tomorrow,' Raphael said. 'Seeing some uni mates in Chelsea. You could come with me? Visit the lawyers. The address is Ebury Street – I could drop you there beforehand.'

Harris wasn't sure. He felt this was a pilgrimage he should make on his own. But this did sound like the quickest way to get answers. And he didn't want to go on wondering what this was about.

'I wouldn't have time to make an appointment,' Harris said.

Raphael made a dismissive noise. 'Oh, just say you dropped by on the off chance. They'll probably want to get it out of the way and off their desks, too.'

When Harris didn't answer, Raphael sighed and dropped the letter down on the bed. 'We'll leave at 9am and you can call them beforehand if you want to. Or don't come. Up to you.'

Harris did phone the firm before, while Raphael was waiting on the drive. He did try to ask the secretary for some details but she said she didn't have them to hand but he was welcome to see Mr Booth from 11am onwards.

Throughout the journey, Raphael was quite talkative. He initially talked about his university friend, Alfred, who was 'making it big' in surveillance technologies, selling big contracts for his products to security companies. Harris didn't have that much interest in covert CCTV cameras or sales figures for such items, but he started to listen more when the conversation turned to the subject of Lauren. Though he asked Harris how he thought the meal with Lauren had gone and what Harris had thought of her, Raphael didn't wait for the answers. Instead, he ploughed on with an extended list of everything that was 'completely amazing about her' until eventually Harris asked, 'Don't you find it a bit awkward telling me about all this?'

'Why?' Raphael said, still sounding casual, although Harris saw a new tension in his face.

'Why do you think?' Harris said, sighing.

Raphael fell silent. He didn't talk for the rest of the drive. Only when they turned down Ebury Street in central London did he ask, 'What number is it?'

'Just drop me here, I'll find it,' Harris said.

'Suit yourself.' Raphael flicked on the indicator and pulled up at the side of the road outside a small bookshop and Harris got out. Raphael drove off without saying goodbye.

Harris felt even more troubled as he walked along the empty street. Had he been unfair? Surely Raphael would know it would make Harris feel odd to hear about his romantic and/or sex life after what had happened between them two years before. The threats Raphael had made at the time – that he would tell his parents that it was Harris who had tried it on with him and that they would throw him out as a result – had seemed more empty as the months and years went by. It had become this silent, secret thing. Impossible to talk about, but also impossible to ignore.

Harris was so caught up in his thoughts he almost walked past the building he needed. He walked up the two steps to the front door and went inside. The secretary – presumably the woman he had spoken to on the phone earlier – seemed surprised he had come alone, but showed him to a chair and offered him some water or a hot drink, which he declined. He was then shown into a clean, minimalist office.

Janson Booth was just as he remembered: a tall, middle-aged man with a stoop and greying hair – perhaps a little more grey than it had been the first time they'd met. He welcomed Harris in and thanked him for coming so quickly. 'I hope it wasn't too much bother you coming to London, but I do prefer the personal touch, and I rather feel it's better to do things face to face when it's concerning a bereavement.' He opened a drawer and took out a black folder. Inside this he brought out a white envelope. 'This is a letter your mother has written to you. She sent it with some other, more routine, legal documents when she completed her will. It was her instruction that, in the event of her death beforehand, it should be given to you on your eighteenth birthday.' He held it out.

Harris reached forward and took it. 'Do you know what's inside it?' he asked, turning it over in his hands. It wasn't very thick. The contents could only be a page or two, not much more.

'I have no idea,' Booth said, 'but I thought I'd give you the chance to open it here, just in case there were any legal vagaries or issues that I might be able to help with. It's quite possible you'll have no questions, but I'm here if you need me.'

Harris nodded, still looking at the letter. After a pause, Mr Booth said, 'Of course, you're also very welcome to take it away with you.'

Harris paused. Then he tore open the seal of the envelope and pulled out the pages.

'I'll give you a moment to read it.' Mr Booth smiled, getting up and going out of a door behind his desk.

Harris read through, his eyes growing wide, his mind not fully able to comprehend what he was seeing. Words entered his brain and hit home, but his sense of order, his ability to compute, was quickly being dimmed by a rush of shock and emotion. When Mr Booth came back, he paused, then sat down slowly and quietly, peering at Harris with a look of concern on his face. 'I hope the contents aren't too upsetting,' he said, then when he got no reply he continued, 'can I call someone for you? Your adopted parents, perhaps?'

'No,' Harris said, getting up. 'No, it's ... it's all fine. Thank you for ... for giving me this. Is there anything else?'

Mr Booth said there were just a couple of forms to sign, which Harris did and then left without saying much else.

Harris roamed the streets of London. He wasn't far from his old home on Ecclestone Square, so he walked there and stood outside the house, watching from across the road near the garden gates as a woman supervised an Ocado delivery man carrying in her shopping. 'No not there, bring the frozen crate into the kitchen,' she said in an impatient voice. The driver mumbled something and lifted the plastic crate up higher to go inside. Harris's eyes connected with the woman for a moment and he saw her back away. She seemed unnerved to see him staring at her and he dimly realised it must look a bit odd. A random teenage boy she didn't know, probably pale from shock, surveying her house. How was she to know it had once been his home? His place of safety? Somewhere he thought he'd live all his life. If only he'd known how stable that life he knew was. A life he'd taken for granted. A life that had been extinguished so quickly. The woman broke eye contact, bending down to stop a small boy from running out of the house, his face breaking out into laughter as she caught him in her arms. They then went back inside and closed the door.

He felt drained and exhausted and, passing a Premier Inn, he decided to go inside. On the off-chance, he asked at the desk if they had a room, but they said they were fully booked, so he slumped in one of the sofas in the front foyer and took out the letter again. Before he could start a second read through, the man at the desk came up to him and said they'd just had a cancellation and would he still like a room? Harris nodded and was given a keycard for a small bedroom on the first floor. Once inside, he hastily removed his coat, kicked off his shoes, and sat on the bed cross-legged, laying out each of the letter's pages in front of him. Then he read, carefully and precisely, forcing himself to take in every word and what it meant. How it reshaped his past. How it changed his future.

My Darling Harris,

I really hope you never have to read this letter. I'm only writing it now as I was reading a magazine article about a family who made strange decisions in their wills and their relatives were puzzling for ever after (with important things they should have been told!), so I decided to lay out some things here for you so you won't be in a similar situation. It does involve some awkward details, for which I apologise, my love. But I think it's better for you to know rather than remain in the dark. These are things I plan to tell you myself one day, when you're old enough. So I'm considering this letter as a safety net, a plan B, just in case that isn't possible at any point. Again, I really hope this isn't needed, but you never know what life might throw at you. I'm resisting writing anything too emotional about having to miss you growing up/getting married etc. Perhaps it would be different if I was dying of an illness, but since I'm fighting fit and hopefully will be long into your middle-age and beyond, I can't help feel this is all a bit unnecessary. But it will give me peace of mind to know that it's all written down here just in case.

So – hypothetical time! Presuming your father and I are no longer here, and such a terrible incident happened before you reached adulthood, you'll have gone to live with the Moncrieff family. I'm sorry it couldn't be with a family you knew better, but your father and I were never ones to have lots of friends who could offer you a home (the other candidates were our friends, the Medlows but after their rather embarrassing legal issues I couldn't really approach them). But I am confident the Moncrieffs will take you in and give you every advantage in life. They have their faults (I'll get to that, believe me) but they are very generous with their money and have more than enough to spare.

Here we get to the big headlines, my love. And I'm so, so

sorry this is how you're finding out. Patrick Moncrieff is your biological father. I was having an affair with him when I became pregnant with you and the dates fit. Mine and your dad's dates, on the other hand – well they don't fit at all. No child wants to hear about 'that side of things' when it comes to their parents, but just know that I don't think it would have been possible for you to be your dad's son. He didn't seem any the wiser, but I did the mathematics over and over again. And we had been trying for a long time without luck. I'm not making excuses, but trying for a baby without results is hard on a couple. Things became tough between us. I met Patrick Moncrieff through work and we became friends – then more than friends. Please try not to judge me. Because if that hadn't happened, I would never have had you. My beautiful, wonderful boy. So I don't write this with too much regret, you understand. I love your father, but sometimes mistakes or errors can also lead to wonderful things.

My affair with Patrick was, to put it simply, a bit odd. Complicated, would be an easy way of saying it. He was always very generous with money and offered a lot to me. And I took it. Rightly or wrongly, I allowed him to bankroll a lot of my existence. Your father didn't know, which meant I spent many years lying to him about my own wealth, telling him my money came from a distant relative. He has always been terribly scatterbrained when it comes to finances and I'm sorry to say that it was easy to deceive him. An uncharitable reading of this whole messy situation could be that I was being paid for my company – a certain kind of company, if you see what I mean (I'm sorry, my love, I realise this must be embarrassing, I'll try to be brief on this side of things). Patrick Moncrieff was, and no doubt still is, a complex man. There were some things he did that upset me, some aspects of his character that concerned me, but I am in no doubt that he and his wife Isabelle will provide you with the best set-up in life for your future, as opposed to an underfunded children's home. I couldn't cope with the thought of you cast off into the world.

There is one other thing I thought I should mention to you. I've had a bit of indecision about this bit, since one could argue it's none of my business, but I've decided to keep it in. You have another half-brother. Raphael Moncrieff, of course, is your half-brother, but there is another. This takes some explaining. One day, years ago, I followed Patrick in London after one of our meet-ups and found that he was having another affair with a woman named Georgia in Clapham, although he seemed to be keeping her in far less comfortable circumstances compared with my own. I engineered a friendship with this woman and discovered she too has a son although she was cagey about who the father was. We remained friends, although I never let on that I knew Patrick was the father of both our sons. So that is why I've decided to include this here: I want to put this right. Your brother is named Rhys Clarkson and at the time of writing this letter, he lives in Clapham. You may wish to contact him some day. How and if you decide to tell him about this (presuming he doesn't know already) will be up to you.

I hope this doesn't come as too much of a shock to you.
You may know a lot of it already. You may dislike me after
finding out what I've done, the secrets I've held so close, the
betrayals I've kept from view. Only know that I'm sorry and
I love you.

Have a wonderful life, my love,
Mum

Once he'd finished reading the letter, Harris put the
pages neatly back into the envelope, got off the bed and
went to sit on the little chair by the desk in the room. He
felt tears stinging his eyes. He let them fall, but didn't
break into sobs. His thoughts were in too much turmoil
to allow for proper crying. Too much was up in the air.
Too many ideas were whirring, colliding. He felt stupid
for never guessing that Patrick was his real father. He felt
betrayed for being made to believe his dad – or the man
he always thought was his dad – was no blood relation.
Did it matter? Did this change anything? Then he
thought about what she'd said about brothers. Raphael
… and this other boy, Rhys.

When his thoughts turned to Raphael, he suddenly
felt sick.

Memories of what had happened between them
flooded his mind. What they'd done. Two brothers,
together. The nausea became a reality. He dashed to the
en suite and vomited into the sink. Feeling dizzy and
worse than before, he collapsed on the hard bathroom

floor and stayed there, tucking himself into a small ball, clutching at one of the towels, pulling it down over him. He lay there for hours and only unfurled himself when he felt his phone buzzing. Raphael was calling.

Harris didn't answer. A few moments later a message arrived, with Raphael asking if he wanted picking up, saying he could come round to Ebury Street if Harris was still around there. It appeared Harris had been forgiven for the tense moment in the car earlier. Part of Harris couldn't bear the thought of travelling with Raphael all the way back to Bath. But he didn't fancy getting a train, either. So he messaged to say to pick him up outside the Premier Inn on Gillingham Street.

Harris paid for the room, ignoring the confused looks on the receptionist's face as he did so, then went outside to wait for Raphael. When he arrived, he got in the car without saying anything. It felt very strange, seeing this boy – or young man, as he was now, knowing he was a relation. A sibling. Someone Harris was connected to by blood. And how it just placed complication upon complication, creating havoc amidst his already confused feelings towards him.

'All right?' asked Raphael, eyeing him suspiciously, 'you look ... well, awful. What did the lawyer say to you?'

'It was nothing,' Harris said. 'Just ... just paperwork for ... a bit of extra cash for university.'

'Thought it would be,' Raphael said, nodding. He was

still looking at Harris, clearly unsettled by the boy's red eyes and pale complexion, and only moved off when a taxi driver beeped at him from behind.

Raphael spent most of the journey back either in silence or making inane conversation about things Harris didn't care about – mostly to do with Lauren, about when Raphael was next seeing her and how he hoped the earrings he'd bought her in Harrods would be to her liking. Harris let it all wash over him, offering minimal engagement in return. Only when they pulled up outside the house a few hours later did Raphael ask him 'Are you going to tell my dad about the money?'

Harris turned in his seat to look at him, his neck clicking through lack of movement. He thought how strange it was to hear Raphael say '*my* dad'. He always had, when talking to Harris, added that possessive word before 'dad' or 'mum' or 'father' or 'mother', but now it seemed particularly loaded. Harris opened his mouth and for a second he thought he might just tell Raphael everything, spill all the seconds, let it all out and change his half-brother's world, just as his had been changed mere hours earlier. But instead he just said, 'No. I'm not going to tell him anything.'

Raphael frowned, but then shrugged. 'Suit yourself,' he said for the second time that day, and got out of the car.

Chapter Twenty-Seven

HARRIS

Seven months before the party

The Moncrieffs had expressed surprise when Harris said he wanted to apply for a degree in London, rather than go off to Cambridge or Oxford (which had both been on Raphael's list). The truth was, Harris thought it unlikely any application to those establishments would be successful. His grades were generally very high, but he didn't relish the thought of the cut-throat interview process, and nothing about those places appealed as much to being back in the city he'd once called home. He'd worried that living back in London would be painful, but was glad he hadn't let this deter him. The sense of familiarity and times gone by was difficult at first, but Harris ended up finding comfort in such feelings and was soon sure he had made the right choice. And he wasn't just in the capital to study. He had other ideas in mind.

Once he had settled into the small but luxurious flat Patrick had provided, he set to work putting into plan his real reason for choosing a London campus. It hadn't taken long to find him online. Rhys Clarkson. A student at the Jesper Ven Torro College of Technology & Computing Science. His relatively unique name was a blessing. And once he'd done his digital research, Harris switched to the outside world. He waited outside the JVT College main building for a week, hoping to see Rhys. On day three of that week, he was successful. He worried it would be a long shot, but on a cloudy Tuesday at the end of September, whilst sipping a Starbucks' Pumpkin Spice Latte, Harris saw him. He knew it the instant the boy came round the corner. He was on his own, dressed in black skinny jeans and a thick, dark green hoodie. Airpods in his ears. Dark frizzy hair. A kind face. Could Harris see a resemblance between them? He wasn't sure. Perhaps there was. Perhaps he was imagining it because of what he knew.

As he walked past Harris, he saw the boy's eyes, for the briefest of moments, connect with his. He felt a jolt within him. Rhys smiled. A pleasant, generous expression, considering he was looking at a stranger. Then he was gone, walking through the doors. Harris thought about this close encounter for the rest of the day while he attended his own classes just over a mile away.

While he was supposed to be analysing a key chapter in Charlotte Bronte's *Villette*, his mind was over in Tottenham Court Road, where his half-brother would be sitting at his laptop learning to code or hack or design, or whatever it was technology students did. The main difference, of course, was that Rhys almost definitely wasn't thinking about him. Rhys didn't know he passed a blood relative on a busy road in Central London earlier. Or did he? Was there something – some inner feeling – that connected siblings, or close family members, so that they always knew, deep down? Harris thought back to the day he'd met Raphael. Did he know then? Could he sense it? He didn't think so. Then, of course, there was the thorny issue of what had happened between him and Raphael. He had gone from feeling horrified and repulsed about what they'd inadvertently done, to settling on a vague decision not to be too hard on himself about it. He hadn't known. Neither of them had. And leaving aside his anger at Raphael for the threats and blackmail that had come the next morning, he found it easier to chalk the experience up to, well, experience and leave it at that. But while sitting in his English seminar thinking about the connection he felt to Rhys, he wondered if maybe what he and Raphael had done had been, in some ways, a version of that. A deep, charged feeling of connection that they hadn't been able to avoid, like two magnets drawn together without understanding the whys and hows. He remembered reading about the many examples of siblings who had accidentally ended up in relationships – even marrying each other and having families before realising – and knew that some scientists, theorists, psychologists and other experts had hypothesised that there was something that drew siblings together without them being entirely aware it was happening.

Harris wasn't successful in seeing Rhys for another two days. Then, on the Friday, standing outside the JVT building as afternoon turned into evening, he bumped into Rhys again. Literally bumped into him. He'd turned to go, deciding to give up for the day, when they collided just as Rhys went to use the pelican crossing to switch over to the other side, his eyes on his phone.

'Shit, sorry man,' he said, looking up briefly. He then crossed the road, not looking back.

And Harris followed.

Rhys walked down the road and turned off to go down Denmark Street. He went into a Boots and came out six minutes later holding a sandwich and a bottle of Pepsi Max. Then he continued down the street until it led up to an intersection with Shaftsbury Avenue. Harris continued to follow him until the boy went into a film and music shop at the lower end of the road. Harris paused for a moment, and then followed him inside.

He couldn't see Rhys at first, then realised there was a basement floor and went downstairs. He found him perusing a shelf of films towards the back of the shop near the counter. Harris wasn't sure if he intended to speak to him or just watch and continue to wait. But he was spared making a decision when Rhys turned around and looked straight at him. In his eyes was something that alarmed Harris. Something like fear and anger mixed together.

'Okay, sorry, this can't be a coincidence,' he said in a loud, carrying voice, 'why are you following me?'

Panic flooded through Harris and he looked around him, hoping to have something nearby – perhaps a rack of Japanese Martial-Arts-themed Blu-rays or the shelf of science-fiction posters – to use as a valid excuse; perhaps he could pretend he was here to pick up a massive, printed sheet featuring the faces of Agents Moulder and Scully and leave quickly. But he realised immediately this wouldn't work. He had been caught and he needed to explain, somehow, the reasons behind all this or potentially miss his chance. Be labelled a stalker, a weirdo, an obsessive best avoided.

'Hi...'

'Hello,' Rhys said, slowly. 'I asked you why you've been following me? I saw you hanging outside my uni the other day, then again from the window yesterday, then I bumped into you on the street half an hour ago. I didn't realise at first until I walked off, but then I joined the dots and realised you'd been hanging around most of the week. And now you're here, in the same shop as me, in an area of London that probably has more retail establishments put together than anywhere in the UK? I don't buy it as a coincidence. So I want to know.'

'I'd ... just seen you ... and wanted to chat...' Harris was aware this didn't make the whole situation sound any better than it was. Rhys clearly looked more unnerved.

'Wanted to chat? What for?'

Harris opened his mouth, then realised he was woefully unprepared to navigate this conversation. He put his hand in his pocket, feeling the letter there, pressed into his pocket, making his leg feel warm. He wondered if he should bring it out now, show it to this boy, tell him what he knew. He wondered if he, too, would feel his whole world alter – if standing here, in a shop, confronted with a stranger, he would come to confront a whole new side of his life's story – his origin story – that he never knew existed.

'I'm ... waiting,' Rhys said, his eyes wide. 'Look, man, is this a ... a hook-up, thing? Because if it is, you should know I'm straight.'

'This isn't anything ... this isn't that sort of thing,' Harris said, managing to get the words out. 'But I would like ... I'd like to talk. Maybe go for a coffee.'

Rhys frowned. 'No, mate, I'm good, thanks.' Then he dodged around Harris and walked back through the shop and upstairs towards the exit.

'Fuck.' Harris cursed himself as he stood there, alone.

He became aware of the shop assistant stickering items by the counter, watching him.

The guy set his stack of DVD boxsets to the side and asked, 'Do you need any help at all?' He made the words sound a bit accusatory and Harris wondered if he'd been eavesdropping on the whole exchange and had formed his own assumptions about what was happening.

'No,' Harris said. 'I'm leaving.'

The shop assistant folded his arms and watched until Harris had left. Once he was outside the shop on Shaftsbury Avenue, Harris scanned the bustling hoards of commuters and tourists and shoppers. By some miracle, his eyes settled on Rhys; he was waiting to cross over at the bottom of the road where Seven Dials, Covent Garden, Soho and the road to Leicester Square and Charring Cross all met. He watched as the lights turned red for traffic and the green man signalled the pedestrians over. Rhys, holding on to his rucksack straps, made his way over to the side of the road where people were waiting outside the theatre for *Harry Potter and the Cursed Child*.

Harris ran. Diving across the road, he was nearly hit by a cyclist who yelled angrily, 'Watch it!' but made it to the other side just before Rhys disappeared round a side street to the right of the Palace Theatre, leading into the depths of Soho. Once he'd gained some distance on him, Harris purposefully held back, catching his breath. He realised that being caught running after Rhys like a madman probably wouldn't help the situation – not that 'the situation' had been very well handled by him up to this point.

Harris followed Rhys down Romilly Street, then up Greek Street. He wondered where the boy was going – perhaps he was meeting friends for dinner here, or going to have drinks. He did indeed stop outside a bar; a rather seedy-looking establishment called 'Club Pleasure', although he didn't go inside. Instead, he took out a key and unlocked the door to the left of the club. The door had peeling brown paint and a mark where the number of the address had clearly once been – Harris could just about make out a '5' but that was about it. He stood there for a long time, his hand once again going to the letter in his pocket. Then he turned away.

He ended up wandering Soho, not wanting to go back to his flat in Southwark, but at the same time feeling uncomfortable amidst the awakening West End nightlife starting to thrive around him. He ended up getting a table for one in Nando's, and ordered a large bowl of Peri Salted Fries, staring out of the window, watching groups of friends walking along, laughing and shrieking. Harris suddenly felt very alone. Alone, even though the restaurant was packed with loudly talking couples and families fresh from the surrounding theatres or cinemas having a bite to eat before getting the train home.

Eventually, after his empty bowl had been cleared by a waiter and he couldn't stomach any more refills of his unlimited soft drink, Harris made a decision. He got up quickly before he could change his mind. Walked the short distance down the street. Found his way back to 'Club Pleasure' and the little door next to it. Then knocked sharply.

The door was opened by a guy wearing faded blue jeans and no top, with a tattoo of a knife-skewered dragon emblazoned over his skinny torso. He was holding a thick joint in one of his hands and exhaled a puff of it before he said in a thick accent which Harris guessed was Russian, 'What you want? You Nev? You here for Eddie? He busy.' Harris told him he wasn't Nev and didn't know who Eddie was. He was here for Rhys.

'Rhys? Really? Er... Okay, yeah man, sure, come up.' Harris followed. The scent of cannabis became stronger as soon as he stepped inside. It seemed to envelope him like a toxic mist, making Harris feel instantly nauseous. He could hear a mixture of sounds – music, with a steady constant beat that seemed at odds with another beat that was causing the floor to pulsate, presumably from the club next door and possibly below, too, if it had a basement level. Mingled with this was the unmistakable moaning and grunting sound of sexual activity, along with someone shouting 'Fucking quality, mate, fucking *quality!*' The corridor was dark with a single flickering bulb giving the whole place an eerie feel. Even if it hadn't been from the disorientating sounds and scent of illegal substances, the whole look of the peeling wallpaper and poor lighting would have signalled to Harris that this was not a place he wanted to be. Why was Rhys here? He wondered for a moment if he'd got the wrong door?

'Rhys, yeah?' the guy says, sniffing loudly and rubbing his nose and reminding Harris that no, he hadn't got the wrong door. 'This way. Upstairs, man, upstairs.'

Harris nodded and started to follow the man. A room to his left had its door open, just before the stairs, and Harris glanced in to see a windowless room with an unclothed couple entwined on a bed, the man kissing the woman's breasts. He looked up as Harris passed but he didn't look annoyed or even interested – his eyes were vacant. Then Harris saw the phone on the tripod at the end of the bed, hooked up to a laptop.

'Best not disturb them, man, they're streaming,' the man on the stairs said. 'Come, follow, I'll get you to Rhys.'

Leave now, a voice said in Harris's said. *This isn't the sort of place you want to be. Leave now.*

But he didn't leave. He continued to follow.

At a small landing, Harris's guide stuck his head round a door, looked inside, came out looking confused. Then he said 'Ah,' and opened another. The sound of water gushing became audible.

'Rhys?' the man said, going partly inside.

'Be out in two mins, mate,' came a voice from within. Rhys's voice, Harris was sure.

'Rhys showers right now,' the man said,

withdrawing. 'You come wait inside here,' he continued, nodding Harris forward. They went through into what appeared to be an upstairs lounge with a large, tatty sofa up against the wall. A large window looked out to the nearby brick-wall of another building with a red, neon sign to the side which said 'ADULTS ONLY' in a curling font, the red glow of it shining through the window and mixing with the harsh fluorescent light on the ceiling. A TV was on, playing what appeared to be a music video channel, the image pixelated and the sound distorted. There were four other people in the room. In the corner on a single-seater chair that didn't match the main sofa was a young guy, probably around Harris's age or slightly older, lying back with his jeans bunched around his ankles, one hand holding onto the chair behind him and the other resting on a young woman's head which was moving in his lap. The girl kneeling between his legs was naked and Harris was disturbed to see deep cuts down her back – some of them scars, some of them barely-healed wounds. The cuts seemed to mingle with a shape of some kind, something that appeared to shift and shimmer, and as he continued to watch he saw it was a tattoo of a shell with a mother-of-pearl effect apparently inked into its structure. The two others in the room – two other young men, both in matching London T-shirts of the type tourists buy – were crouched in front of a coffee table with a smudged glass top. Along with the remnants of paper containing chips and half-eaten pizza, Harris could see a large quantity of white powder and what appeared to be prescription pill bottles.

'Take a seat, friend,' Harris's guide said. 'Rhys be out in very short time, okay? You college friend?'

Harris nodded, rendered speechless by all the things he'd seen in the short space of time between knocking on the door and sitting down on the creaking faux leather sofa.

'You want beer?' the man said. 'Or some...' He nodded at the coffee table. One of the men had gathered a quantity of pills in front of him and was in the process of crushing them to dust underneath the base of a heavy glass tumbler. They then used what looked like a straw from a juice carton to snort the crushed powder into their noses.

'No,' Harris said, quickly. 'I ... I don't think ... I think this is a mistake.' He went to get up but the guy shoved him down, a little roughly.

'No, man, you sit, I get Rhys for you. You're welcome, man. Friend of Rhys, friend of ours.'

There was a sudden loud gasp and a moan and the man in the corner chair punched the air enthusiastically with a clenched fist. 'Fucking gold, love, fucking gold.' The woman raised her head and backed out from between his legs. Her eyes were half shut, as if she was close to passing out. The young man got unsteadily to his feet and came straight over to the table. 'Fucking buzzing after that,' he said. He sounded Scottish, his eyes wide and manic, and he bounced up and down on the balls of his bare feet as his two friends on the floor cut him a line of powder, which he bent down to sniff.

The girl opened her eyes more fully, blinked a little, looked at the activities happening around the table and decided to join in, although she seemed nowhere near as enthusiastic. Harris thought it likely she was already on something and he felt a sudden need to ask her if she was okay, if she was here by her own volition. The guy in the jeans seemed to have noticed Harris staring at her as he reached forward to nudge Harris playfully on the arm and said 'She good, *really* good. You want blow job, yes? She give good BJ. Very good. She give you while you wait?'

Harris shook his head.

'Ah, you miss out, man,' he said, giving a sharp laugh. Harris continued to stare at the woman. He thought of dark, unsettling possibilities – that she may have been kidnapped, drugged and brought here; sex trafficked, perhaps? Or, so far into the depths of addiction that she no longer knew or cared about her surroundings and the company she was keeping. He opened his mouth, unsure what he wanted to say just that he had to say something, but no words were coming out. Meanwhile, one of the London T-shirt men brought out a spoon and arranged something on its surface, then placed a syringe down next to it.

'What the fuck?' said a voice to his left. He looked

round and saw Rhys standing there. His dark hair was damp and he was bare-chested, wearing pyjama bottoms with the Batman logo dotted over them. He had a small towel slung over his shoulder, water still dripping into it as he stood there, looking at Harris in consternation.

'Hi,' Harris said. It was all he could manage in that moment.

'This is ... getting too weird,' Rhys said, staring at him.

'Sorry, I...' Harris stood up, feeling a little shaky.

'He your friend, yes,' the jeans guy said animatedly. He'd sunk down on the single-seater and was now flicking through TV channels using a broken remote, jabbing it at the screen when it refused to respond.

Rhys stared over at him. 'No, not my friend. He's a stalker.'

'I'm not a stalker,' Harris said.

A tense silence followed, broken only by the occasional sharp sniff from the coffee table. Then the tattoo man said, 'You want me to throw him out on his arse, yes? Chuck him into the street?' He cracked his knuckles.

'Please don't,' Harris said, stepping forward. 'Please, Rhys, can we just go and talk somewhere? Do ... do you have a bedroom here?' Harris reached into his pocket and brought out the crumpled envelope. 'There's something I need to show you. I was ... trying to tell you earlier. It's important.'

Rhys looked at him for a few seconds more. Then nodded. 'Okay. But if this is some wind-up or you're a nutter or something, you'll … you'll be sorry,' he finished, a little pathetically. 'Come on, this way.'

He led the way out of the living room and along the landing to one of three other doors. On stepping inside, Harris felt he had stepped into another building – or even another world altogether. The difference to the room he had just exited was extraordinary. Rhys's bedroom was homely and, from the looks of it, a very comfortable, calm oasis from the horrors going on outside it. The bed, though a small single, was neatly made with a thick-looking duvet contained within in a DC Superhero-themed cover with matching pillows. A very soft-looking grey throw was folded along the end of the bed. There was a desk with two computer monitors and a laptop, along with a stack of textbooks, a pencil case and some notepads. A shelf above the desk sported more books – novels, it seemed, mostly video-game or movie tie-ins and whole sets of fantasy works from authors like J.R.R. Tolkien, J.K Rowling and C.S. Lewis. A trail of fairy lights was strung along the shelf, illuminating the volumes with a warm glow. The room wasn't artificially pristine – he could see a laundry basket that was in danger of overflowing, some socks and shirts that had evidently been discarded on the floor by the bed, a collapsing tower of computer games and ring-binder folders in the corner. But the overall effect was of a homely, welcoming environment. And Harris found it strangely moving.

'Why are you staring?' Rhys asked. 'What is this about?'

'This room … it's so different to…'

Rhys sighed. 'Yeah, well… I think I have different tastes to my flatmates.' He walked over to a small chest of drawers by the bed, pulled out a white T-shirt and tugged it on. 'Now, tell me what this is all about. You're kind of freaking me out, you know. I don't know why I brought you in here. Well, yeah, I do, I didn't want Spiker punching your lights out.'

'He'd do that?' Harris asked, a little shakily.

'He's done a lot worse,' said Rhys. 'Now come on, I'm not going to ask you again. Explain.'

Harris took a deep breath. 'We're related.'

Rhys stared back at him. Then he laughed. 'Sorry mate, but I really don't think—'

'We are. We have the same father. His name is Patrick Moncrieff. I'm … I'm your brother.'

Chapter Twenty-Eight

HARRIS

Seven months before the party

It took some time for Rhys to come around to the idea that he and Harris were related. He seemed reluctant to even entertain the possibility. But the letter changed everything. He read it, his eyes growing wide as they moved across the page. Then, to Harris's surprise and alarm, they seemed to fill with tears. After finishing, he'd silently handed the letter back to Harris and exited the room. Harris stood there, unsure what to do. Then he reached down, took off his trainers, put them neatly by the door, and went to sit down on the bed. He could feel the distant thudding beat of music causing the frame to vibrate a little. He sat there for a good five or ten minutes before Rhys returned. His eyes looked red and a little puffy. It was obvious he'd been crying. He looked at

Harris sitting on the bed, waited a moment, then walked over to join him. He sat at the top end nearest the pillows, pulling himself up to sit cross-legged. Then he asked Harris to explain his side of everything.

Harris told him all that he knew. That his mother and father had lived in a house in Ecclestone Square that turned out to be owned by Patrick Moncrieff, who had met Harris's mother through work, had begun an affair with her, and then she'd fallen pregnant. Patrick had wanted her to get an abortion, but she'd refused. He threatened to tell her husband everything, but never did, and didn't want a relationship with Harris. But because she didn't have any money of her own, in the event of her death if he was still a child she had arranged for him to be taken in by the Moncrieffs. And still Patrick had chosen to keep it a secret. It was only when Harris had received the letter when he turned eighteen, that he'd discovered the truth.

'Have you confronted him?' Rhys asked. 'You must have been tempted. After you read all that.'

Harris shook his head. 'Part of me wants to wait. To see if he acknowledges it without me having to force the truth out of him. I doubt he's told his wife, she wasn't wild about me living with them when I was a charity case, so she'd probably hit the roof if she found out I was a child her husband had through an affair.'

'And the boy … your brother. Half-brother. Our half-brother? What about him?'

'Raphael? I don't think he knows. In fact, I'm pretty sure he doesn't otherwise he wouldn't have...'

'Wouldn't what?'

Harris sighed. 'Things involving Raphael are ... complicated. They're ... it's ... just a bit complicated...'

Rhys looked interested but didn't ask Harris to explain, so Harris stayed silent. Then Rhys said, 'What do you think of Patrick?'

Harris frowned. 'As in, do I like him?'

'Yeah,' Rhys said. 'Like ... I know he had an affair with your mum but it doesn't seem...' He paused, taking a deep breath. Whatever he was trying to ask seemed to be difficult for him. 'She didn't ... she sounded like he was an okay guy with her. Like, she didn't mind putting him and his wife down as the people to look after you if anything happened to her and your dad, so I suppose he wasn't ... like, nasty, or anything to her?'

Harris thought back to his mother's words. He looked at the folded letter on the surface of the bed. He didn't need to open it to re-read it – he had almost memorised it by heart, having read it over and over, again and again, savouring the sudden connection with the past its arrival had offered.

'She mentioned she didn't love him like she loved my dad. But then again, I suppose ... there must have been some difficulties with my father I didn't know about, if she felt the need ... if she continued having an affair...

And he's been all right to me. Actually, he's been nicer to me than the others.'

'He isn't a nice man.'

Rhys said the sentence with a certainty that made Harris look up quickly.

'What? What do you mean? I thought you...'

'I don't know him, no. Not like that. Well, not personally. But ... in some ways ... I do know him. Or I think I do.'

'That doesn't make any sense,' Harris said, readjusting his sitting position on the bed, sitting up straighter.

Rhys sighed heavily. 'I'm sorry, it's just ... these memories are rather difficult for me.'

'Well ... take your time,' Harris said, noticing how upset Rhys looked but at the same time eager to get answers.

'I need to check something.' He took out his phone and typed away for a moment. Then his eyes widened as he stared at the screen. Scrolled for a bit. Paused. Then he laid the phone down on the bed, clicking the screen off.

'What were you checking?'

Rhys didn't answer straight away. He chewed his bottom lip for a few seconds. Blinked hard for a bit. Then he began. 'When I was boy ... as early as I can remember ... a man used to visit my home. I was in a tiny flat with my mum. She was a cleaner, didn't earn much money at all. It was pretty desperate at times, I think. Then for a while it would be a little less desperate. A bit more money, a bit more food. Those times always...' he paused and swallowed, 'they always coincided with a visitor coming to the flat. A man. I was never allowed to see him. I was told to keep quiet and stay in my room. I was not to come out or make any noise. I was told it was very important. And I was a good kid. I always did as I was told. I... I was terrified. I'd hide under my duvet, burying my head in the pillows, counting down from a hundred, then again from two hundred. Or I'd go through all the characters in every story I'd heard, every book I'd read, every film I'd seen. Or sometimes I was too upset or scared to do any of that and I'd just try to lie still. I thought the man must be a really bad man if Mum made me hide. And I'd hear things. Things ... noises. I didn't know what it was at the time. I think I knew it was something ... adult. Something I didn't understand. And then the door would slam. Afterwards I'd hear my mum crying in the other room before she let me out. She'd always try to cover up her tears and make herself look normal, doing her hair nice again, changing her clothes. But sometimes it wasn't possible. She'd ... she'd have bruises. Bruises on her neck, or marks on her cheeks, as if her face had been pushed into the carpet or the wall. Red patches on her arms – particularly her wrists, although if she realised they were there she'd rush to pull on a cardigan to cover them up, even if it was a hot day.'

A small tear trickled out of the corner of Rhys's left

eye. He brushed it away quickly and sniffed. But when he carried on his voice was calm and steady. 'Well, this happened a few times – more than a few. Enough for me to become familiar with it. Although I knew there was something … something terrible going on. And one day I got brave enough to take a look. Not out of the door. I'd already tried that once, against my mum's instructions – I'd tried to open the door. But she'd either locked it or blocked it. But it was the window I looked out of. I made a pile of books and a toy chest thing I had and I managed to balance just high enough to look out the window down at the street. I saw the man come out. I've never forgotten his face. Watching him leave. I've never seen him again. Until today. On this phone.' He unlocked the phone and held it up. A corporate-style photo smiled back from the screen. 'When I googled the name "Patrick Moncrieff".'

Chapter Twenty-Nine

HARRIS

Five months before the party

Harris and Rhys moved in together. The decision was made within a couple of weeks of them meeting. After all, Harris had the space in the small, two-bed apartment Patrick had sorted for him.

'What if he finds out?' Rhys asked, unsure at first.

'He won't,' Harris assured him. 'And if he does, you can just be a friend crashing at my place. We'll say you've had a bad break-up or something. Needed a place to stay. Regardless, I'm not convinced he'd know or care.'

They found they had an instant liking for each other, an instant bond that shocked Harris with its rich, sudden force. He wondered if this was what some people felt when they fell in love – after all, he did feel like he was falling in love, but not romantic love, a familial love that had been up until now denied to him; a fraternal bond that was so strong he felt very quickly as if it had become a new pillar of his existence.

The revelations Rhys had shared about Patrick Moncrieff and the conversation that followed had in some ways stunned Harris, and in other ways hadn't surprised him at all. When Rhys had struggled to keep his tears back, Harris had put his arms around him and held him close. Rhys had then gone on to explain that his mother had died from an overdose of sleeping pills and Alprazolam when he was twelve. He said he'd gone into care for a bit, then gone to some foster parents. He'd worked hard and secured a grant from a computing-education fund, which is how he could afford to go to university and pay rent.

'Do you think it was suicide?' Harris asked, gently.

Rhys shook his head. 'It's impossible to tell for sure, but I think she just forgot how much she had taken. She had periods when she was very sad and just slept for hours and hours. And on one of these times ... well, she just didn't wake up.'

Harris struggled to control his own emotions when he heard this. He thought of his own parent's death. They'd been barely a mile from their home, travelling in the car on an ordinary day, when a skip came loose from the back of a lorry as it turned onto Lyall Street, and his dad had swerved to avoid it. The car had smashed into some scaffolding and building works outside a block of nearby houses and apartments. Harris told Rhys about his parents' accident and how, soon after he'd arrived back to London a few weeks ago, he'd gone for a walk to the place where it had happened. He thought he'd feel an overwhelming sense of grief or at least something, like when he'd gone to stand outside the house on Ecclestone Square. But he hadn't. It was just a London street. And when he didn't feel anything huge and momentous straight away, he fled, suddenly scared it would catch up with him if he lingered for too long.

Harris made friends in his seminar classes and introduced Rhys to them. He never referred to him as his brother, always as his 'flatmate.' They decided not to be too public about the fact they knew they were related. As the term progressed, Harris did extremely well in his first handful of essays. He enjoyed living with Rhys. He loved being back in London. Things were better than they had been in years.

He was surprised when, at the end of term, in the second week of December, Patrick messaged him to say that he was going to come and get Harris from his flat, rather than send a driver. When traffic delayed Patrick's arrival, Harris told him he'd wait in the Caffè Nero on the corner of the street where he lived. Nearly an hour after Patrick was supposed to arrive, a message pinged on Harris's phone telling him to come outside quickly as Patrick was unable to find a parking space.

Harris looked up from his phone across the table. 'I'd better go,' he said to Rhys, who had accompanied him to the café.

'Good you got a takeaway cup for your third coffee,' he said to Harris. 'Do you need help with your bags?'

'No, no, I'm fine,' Harris said. 'Well, see you in January.' They weren't sure if they should hug – they hadn't quite got their sense of tactile familiarity with each other sorted, so they vaguely patted each others shoulders and arms and Harris exited the coffee shop.

'Who's that?' Patrick asked as Harris got into the car after throwing his rucksack into the seat behind.

'Oh, er, just a friend,' Harris said as they drove off. He looked back at the café and saw Rhys's eyes following them through the glass frontage as they left.

It took Harris a while to realise they weren't driving in the direction of Bath, but heading in the other direction, towards Essex.

'Where … what…?' Harris muttered confusedly, staring at the road signage, then glancing at the screen on the dashboard. The destination was a postcode he didn't recognise.

'We're going on a trip,' Patrick said, sounding in good spirits. 'A pre-Christmas adventure.'

'To Essex?' Harris asked.

'Yes, to the countryside. There's something I want to show you.'

They journeyed on until they reached a sign announcing they were entering the village of Tolleshunt D'Arcy. By this point, the afternoon light was starting to wane and Harris was intrigued when Patrick steered the car off the road and up a private driveway. There was a wooden sign at the entrance that was faded and scratched and some lettering that had presumably, once upon a time, spelled out the name of the house.

'What is this place?' Harris asked, feeling frustrated by the lack of information he was being given. Patrick just smiled and continued to drive the car up the winding driveway, around the bushes and trees until a large house came into view. It looked like a combination of a traditional English country house and something more medieval, with a red-brick frontage that appeared younger than the rest of the building on each side.

'This is a very exciting place. Or at least I hope it will be. An exciting new venture,' Patrick said, undoing his seat belt and opening the car door. Harris got out, too, and followed him up the gravel drive to the front door, where Patrick had paused and was rummaging in his pockets.

'Whose house is this? Is it a house?'

'It's mine,' Patrick said, casually. 'I've just bought it.'

He found what he was looking for – a small silver-coloured key – and unlocked the door. Although the December air outside wasn't warm, it was nothing compared to the chill that greeted Harris as he stepped inside. It was as if the walls were made of ice, locking the freezing air around the once-grand surroundings. Harris looked around him as they walked through the entrance hall into an impressive room with a large staircase and a lot of space, with marks on the floor showing where furniture and a carpet or rug once rested. The overall impression was of a beautiful house left to go to seed. There were even leaves and twigs at the sides of the room and a thick layer of dust was visible on each step of the staircase.

'I'm going to do this place up. Every room, every part of it. And it's going to be yours.' Patrick let his arms fall to his side with a slap, as if he'd made a grand announcement, one he had been building up to.

At first Harris thought he'd misheard him. 'Sorry? What … what do you mean?' he said, looking up.

'It's going to be yours?' said Patrick, grinning at Harris, clearly delighted to be offering this news.

'I … I don't understand. The whole house?'

'Yes,' Harris said. 'You see, you don't know this, but …well … there's a lot you don't know. To start with, you'll know that your parents didn't own your house. They rented it, and I know your mother went with a story about it being owned by a relative in Scotland that she'd fallen out with. I never thought it was that convincing, but your father was terminally incurious and you were, well, too young to question it. But it wasn't owned by any distant relative, it was owned by me. I'm sorry that I couldn't keep that from you, I had to sell it in order to please a particularly demanding client a couple of years ago. So I want to make amends for that. I realise this is, um, a bit different to a London townhouse, but I hope it will be... Well, I hope you make a go of it, once you've graduated and you can set up here yourself.'

Things were starting to slot into place for Harris. As he pulled his gaze away from Patrick's eager expression, he looked around him and realised what he was seeing: not a large country home in need of a paint job. It was guilt. Guilt made manifest.

'That isn't the whole story, though, is it?' Harris said, feeling a prickle of anger on the back of his neck.

'I'm sorry?' Patrick frowned. 'I don't understand.'

'You say my father was terminally incurious,' Harris said, 'which is a bit of a harsh way to talk about my dead dad. Wouldn't you say?'

Regret clouded Patrick's face and he shook his head. 'I'm sorry, I ... I chose my words badly there.'

'Yeah, I think you did,' Harris said, forcing himself to swallow, to keep his words as calmly delivered as possible. 'But I think it's probably true. And it suited you, didn't it? It suited you just fine.'

Patrick's eyes widened a little. 'I don't know what you mean, Harris… I've… I've just told you I'm giving you a house. This massive house. And it will be done up nicely for you. You won't have to do anything, I'll have the work done. I'll sort it all.'

Harris half-laughed, then sniffed, the dust in the place irritating his nose. The more he thought about it, the more crass it all seemed. This massive mansion that could house a school or a retirement home or a hospice, given just to him. He'd never considered himself a socialist or particularly left-wing, but now he understood where such people were coming from. 'Jesus Christ, this place – this is insane. Though fucking typical, when you think about it.'

'What's … what's typical?' Patrick asked, looking stunned.

'Typical that you throw crazy money at a problem in order to keep it boxed up at a manageable distance. That's exactly where you want me isn't it – a manageable distance. Knocking about in a house too fucking big for me so that you can tell yourself you're being *generous*.'

'I *am* being fucking generous, Harris! God, you're not making any—'

'*I'm* not making sense? Are you sure? *Father*?'

Silence dropped between them. A deep, echoey silence, with Harris's final word bouncing off the walls. Then he spoke, stepping closer to the man standing in front of him, feeling like he was seeing him for the first time. 'What? Have I shocked you? That wasn't on your list of things to tell me?'

Patrick was still staring at him. Then he said, quietly, 'You guessed?'

'No,' Harris said. 'I probably should have, but I didn't. I was told. By my mother.'

'I don't understand. You've known all this time?'

'She told me in a letter.'

Patrick continued to stare at him, his face a mixture of confusion and panic. Then his features settled and he nodded. 'Of course. Your meeting with Jason Booth.'

Now it was Harris's turn to be taken aback. 'What ... you knew I saw—'

'Raphael told me you'd been left a bit of money when you turned eighteen. I didn't think your parents had much put away but it made sense.'

Harris rolled his eyes. 'What a surprise that Raphael couldn't keep that to himself. But yes, that's how I got the letter. She said you'd been having an affair and that I'm your son.'

Patrick stayed still for a long time. Now it was the word 'son' which seemed to richochet between them, although Harris was surprised how calm his father appeared. It was as if the tension in his face was quickly ebbing away, replaced by something closer to relief.

'I'm glad you know,' he said, nodding slowly. 'But I ... I just wish you'd told me when you found out. We could have talked it through.'

'Could we? Why talk when you could just give me all this?' Harris said, raising his hands at the walls around him, giving the bottom step of the staircase a sharp kick.

'Harris, I don't think—'

'You *used* her for sex. Then you bought her silence with money and a place to live.'

Patrick let out an astonished laugh. 'Christ, is that what she told you? *Used her*? Grow the fuck up, Harris. It was a reciprocal arrangement. She got exactly what she wanted out of it – an SW1 life, money to buy herself some nice bits on the King's Road while she earned next-to-nothing and her husband brought in less than thirty grand a year. When you think about it that way, you have to ask yourself who was actually using who? And she got an unintended sperm donation from me, which like everything else, worked out well for her considering John was firing blanks. So don't get all high and fucking mighty about shit you don't understand, Harris. You might be an adult now, but when you're my age and you look back, you will be horrified at how little you understood the world. You have *no* idea.'

'I think Isabelle would be pretty interested to hear everything that I know. I might even show her the letter. I'm sure she'd find it fascinating.'

Patrick's eyes narrowed. Harris held his ground, refusing to break eye contact.

'Sorry to take the wind out of your sails, but Isabelle knows.'

Harris thought he felt his heart skip a beat. In the seconds that followed, he cursed himself for not anticipating this. After all, it made sense. Her distant, cool tone with him, her reluctance to ever look him in the eye, her default to ignoring his existence unless she really had to acknowledge him. And then the calm, clinical way she had used him on their fateful trip to America. How unconcerned she had been about his welfare. How calmly she did what she did. Harris recognised her behaviour for what it really was. Vindictive. Resentful. Cruel. But at least he was now clear on the reasons behind it all.

'Ah, I see that doesn't quite fit with your little truth crusade,' Patrick said, smirking. 'Like I said, Harris. You understand so little.'

'I'll still tell people,' Harris said, trying to gain back some command of the situation. 'All your posh fucking friends, Raphael, I'll tell them how you paid a woman for sex and had a secret child with her, I'll even tell everyone about Rhys.'

'Who the fuck is Rhys?' Patrick said.

'Don't pretend,' Harris said.

'I don't know what you're talking about, Harris, and to be honest, I'm too fucking furious with you to carry on this conversation right now, okay. Stop making threats. Do what you want.' He turned to leave. 'Oh and you know what, you can find your own way home from here.

Save you spending too much time with a guy as terrible as me.'

The door thudded closed behind him, causing a small plume of dust to rise around it in the near-darkness. Part of Harris thought this was an empty threat, a gesture of anger, but then he heard the car start up and zoom off on the gravel. He opened the front door in time to see it speeding away down the driveway.

'Fuck,' he said to himself, looking around. The sun was properly setting now, the light outside growing dimmer by the second.

Feeling suddenly very tired, he sat down in the doorway of the house, contemplating his options. In the end, he took out his phone and dialled his most recent contact. 'Hey, it's me. Something weird has happened. I need a favour.'

Chapter Thirty

HARRIS

Five months before the party

While Harris waited for Rhys, he explored the house. He went upstairs and drifted through the bedrooms, looking at the faded wallpaper, the cracked wood of the doors, the occasional piece of art still hung on the walls. To some, an empty, creaking old house like this might be a place of terror, the site of a horror movie or the scene of a terrible crime. But to Harris, he found a sort of comfort in the feeling of a once-great place brought down to something more humble. He perused the shelves in the library, most of them empty aside from a few dusty volumes. An Oxford World's Classics edition of Peter Pan. A copy of *The Go-Between* with the cover torn. Inside he found a bookmark with a small watercolour painting of a fox on the end. It looked hand-painted, and he wondered about the family who'd once lived here. Who might have painted the bookmark, or left the novel half-read? Who once sat in the library, flicking through the pages of their books, escaping into other worlds?

Harris was sitting by the outdoor leaf-covered swimming pool when he heard the distant sound of gravel under car tyres. He made his way back into the house and through to the entrance hall. Rhys had arrived.

'You've got to tell me what's going on,' Rhys said, getting out of the car and shaking his head in confusion as he looked up at the house before him.

'Come inside,' Harris said. 'It's cold.'

'God, it feels even colder in here,' Rhys said, wrapping his coat around him as he stepped into the hall. 'Sorry it took a while. I've never been to this part of Essex. And I was in the middle of something.'

Harris frowned. 'In the middle of what? You said you were seeing that friend of yours, Ivana?'

Rhys looked troubled. 'Ivanka,' he said.

Harris raised his eyebrows, a question on his face. 'Why are you still in touch with her? I thought she was a prostitute or a drug addict, or both.'

'I've been helping her, she's had a tough time. Anyway,' he said, continuing to look round. 'What is this place?'

'It's mine,' Harris said, 'apparently. If I want it. Presuming I haven't ruined my chances.'

'What? Yours? What chances?'

Harris led Rhys to the library where there were still chairs to sit on. They sat down, pulling their coats tightly around them and Harris explained what had happened. Patrick's offer of the house and his promise to do it up for him. And how Harris had seen it for what it truly was: Patrick's attempt to smooth his guilt for the whole situation with Harris's mother.

'How do you know it's guilt?' Rhys asked, frowning.

'What else could it be?'

'Love?' replied Rhys, but Harris couldn't tell if he was serious or not.

He blinked at Rhys in the darkness. 'I can hardly see you. Let's go outside. The moon's out.'

'No way,' Rhys said. 'Hold on.' He walked over to the mantlepiece where there was a candle and a box of matches. 'Spotted these as we came in.' He lit the candle and set it on the ground in front of them. Harris was surprised at how much light it gave off, illuminating Rhys's face before him, although it made the surrounding room appear even darker than it had done before.

'Did you tell him about me?' Rhys asked.

Harris paused, then nodded. 'Well, not exactly. I … mentioned you. But I don't think he knew what I was talking about.'

Rhys nodded. 'Makes sense. Bet it's got him wondering, though.'

'Good. He needs to have a long hard think about everything he's done. About what they've *all* done.' Harris stood up, suddenly feeling energised by a rush of anger. Rage, even. 'All three of them... They just ... use people. Use me. For whatever suits them best in that moment then presume it's all fine, that I'll be grateful, that I can be bought off with an obscenely large house. That I'll nod along, be the good boy, the one that makes them look good for taking in an orphan, so long as I don't say too much or cause them any embarrassment.'

'Sounds like they need taking down a peg or two,' Rhys replied.

'Maybe they do,' Harris said. He started to pace the room in silence.

'What are you thinking?' asked Rhys after a minute or two.

'I'm thinking about a time when I was at school. In Year Seven. In my science class...'

'Go on,' prompted Rhys when Harris tailed off into silence, thinking.

'There were some boys who were ... well, they were just dicks. In PE class they stole my shorts and rugby socks. Threw them behind some lockers that were impossible to move.'

'Boys are going to be dicks.'

'I know, but I don't have to just lie back and take it,

do I? And I didn't. Those same boys used to steal apples from Mr Kelly's science lab. He kept a bowl of them on his desk, it was one of his weird things, he was an odd bloke. I don't think the boys were particularly fond of apples, I think they just liked the idea of stealing from a teacher.'

'Forbidden fruit,' said Rhys, nodding.

'Exactly. Well, the day they stole my PE kit, I went to science early as I couldn't do rugby, and there was a supply teacher setting up the class. I knew if Mr Kelly wasn't in, they'd be bound to take as many apples as they wanted when the teacher wasn't looking. So I poisoned them.'

I heard Rhys laugh. 'What do you mean, poisoned? That's ... that's *weird*. Like fucking Snow White or something?'

'Snow White didn't poison the apple, the witch did.'

'I *know* that,' Rhys said. 'Just ... carry on.'

'I used hydrochloric acid. Just some drops on them. I know it was probably really fucking stupid and I shouldn't have done it, but ... I did and, well, it worked. The idiot guys took the apples when the supply teacher had her back turned. One of them bit into one during class.'

'Oh, shit,' said Rhys, 'they didn't ... they didn't die? Tell me they didn't die?'

Harris paused for enough time to see a look of something on Rhys's face that amused him. A look of genuine concern mixed with something he'd never seen in his brother's eyes. Something resembling fear. At last he said, 'Relax. He just got an irritated tongue and lips. Had to go to the medical room. As did two of his friends who'd snuck apples, too. I don't know if they ever traced it back to the fruit basket or if the boys even told them what they'd been eating, but it was … satisfying to see.'

Rhys frowned at him. 'You have a cruel streak I didn't know about.'

'One man's cruel is another man's justice,' replied Harris, staring defiantly back at Rhys.

'How long are we going to stay here, because I'm really fucking cold,' Rhys said.

'Aren't you interested?' Harris asked, still holding his gaze.

'In what?'

'In doing something … satisfying.'

Rhys didn't say anything for a moment, just chewed the inside of his cheek, a habit Harris had come to associate with Rhys thinking about something. Then finally he said, 'Do you have an idea?'

Harris walked back over to the moth-eaten sofa and sat back down. 'We don't need an idea. We need a plan. A when, a where and a how.'

Chapter Thirty-One

HARRIS

Five months before the party

Patrick, Isabelle and Raphael were all out for a charity Christmas mince pie afternoon followed by evening drinks at another function. It sounded hellish to Harris, plus he wasn't sure if he and Patrick were speaking.

Harris waited until the afternoon before starting on the alcohol, then tried making himself some mulled wine by mixing various drinks and cinnamon sticks. The result was sickly but he drank it anyway before heading up to his room with a whole Panettone he'd found in the larder. He tore handfuls of it off, dipping it in his alcoholic concoction, not caring if he got stains on the bed sheets. He streamed *Home Alone* on his laptop, with a candle named 'Winter's Night', and tried to rekindle feelings of childhood Christmases. But the nostalgia wouldn't come – perhaps it was the alcohol, perhaps it was the row with Patrick and the rising feeling of revenge he'd stoked up during his conversation with Rhys. Whatever it was, he ended up falling asleep in an awkward position, half on top of the Panettone, and only woke up when he began to cough.

Smoke. The end of one of his cushions had fallen over so it was covering the candle. Acting fast, Harris grabbed the pillow by the other end, opened the window and threw it out. He watched as it fell to the ground like a glowing ball and extinguished upon landing.

Turning back to the room, he was relieved to see that the damage was minimal – the wall had been spared of smoke damage, only the headboard of the bed bore marks, and he didn't much care if it was replaced or stayed like that. He looked over at the doorway, where a smoke alarm was fixed on the ceiling. Curious that it hadn't gone off in warning, he dragged his desk chair over and pressed the button on it. Nothing. Peering at it more closely he noticed a hole in the side of the plastic shell. Gripping the sides tightly, he twisted and pulled. And then stared, astonished, at what he saw.

'I need you right now,' Harris said to Rhys on the phone. 'They're out, will be until tomorrow. I've … discovered something. And if I'm right, I'm going to need your tech expertise. This is … is beyond anything.'

Rhys muttered something about how Harris always clicked his fingers and expected him to come running, but Harris could tell his brother was too intrigued to say no. 'I'll be there in a few hours,' Rhys said, then ended the call.

Harris made his way to Raphael's room and found his laptop on the desk. He opened it and wasn't surprised when he was met with the password screen. He went back to his room and stood by the window, thinking. He should probably go out and find the burnt pillow, he thought. A movement caught his attention, distracting him from his thoughts. The gardener's son, Eric. The Moncrieff's had a regular gardener but it wasn't often that he brought his son to help out. Harris could see Eric using a rake to clear leaves from the back lawn, a thankless task given the leaves would just be replaced by the next day. Harris turned and looked over at the smoke detector. Then back out of the window. An idea blossoming in his mind.

Within two minutes, he was making his way across the lawn. Eric had made his way further down the garden towards the annex where he'd gathered the stray leaves into a pile.

'Hey,' Harris said as he approached, 'how's it going?'

He saw the boy shivering, even though he had on a thick jumper and coat. 'Hey,' Eric said back, clearly surprised that Harris was out here talking to him. 'Not bad, thanks ... er ... got a lot of work to do. My dad has the flu so it's just me today. I'm on Christmas break from school, so it works out fine.'

Harris nodded. 'Weird question,' he said, 'but ... how old are you now?'

Eric frowned. 'I'm sixteen, why?'

'Because,' Harris said, taking out his phone and pulling up a dating app. 'I think you're supposed to be eighteen to be on this.'

He watched as the boy turned red. 'Oh ... yeah ... sure ... that's ... I knew that. Don't tell my dad, will you?' he mumbled, letting out an awkward laugh.

'Don't worry, I won't,' Harris said, wrapping his cardigan around him.

'I've ... seen you on there,' Eric said, dropping his gaze a little, clearly embarrassed. But Harris noticed the small smile play on his lips.

'You should have said hi. Or something,' Harris replied, adding weighted pauses between his words.

Eric looked up at him. And Harris stared back. Then he said, 'You know, it's too cold to be working out here. You should come inside. Warm up a bit.'

Eric visibly swallowed, opened his mouth, staring at Harris. 'Warm up ... how?'

Harris just smiled knowingly and turned away making his way back to the main house. 'You coming?' he called back.

He heard the rake fall to the ground. Footsteps followed. Eric was very much coming.

———————

Harris's phone started buzzing at a rather inopportune moment. Eric begged him not to stop what he was doing and Harris continued as he reached over and picked up the phone.

'Hey, I'm outside,' Rhys said.

'Five minutes,' Harris grunted.

'What?'

'I said, give me five minutes.'

Rhys started to say something else, but Harris cut the call.

Five minutes later, panting heavily, Harris climbed off the bed and pulled on his underwear. 'That was good,' he said to Eric, 'let's do it again sometime.'

Without waiting to chat, he walked out the room, down the stairs and opened the front door.

'Finally,' Rhys said, coming up the steps, then raising his eyebrows at Harris's attire. 'What…? Why are you…? Hang on, were you just…'

He didn't need to finish the question as Eric came walking down the stairs, straightening out his T-shirt and zipping up his trousers.

'I'd better get back to work,' Eric said, shooting an

embarrassed half-smile at Rhys. 'I'll ... er, use the kitchen door.' He headed off back through the house.

'Sure,' Harris said, then turned back to Rhys. 'Come on, let's go upstairs.'

'Who was that?' asked Rhys, 'Are you and he a thing?'

'Briefly,' Harris replied.

'So what's this major discovery?' Rhys asked as they climbed the stairs.

He led him into his bedroom. Rhys smirked at the messed-up bed and scattered clothes, but said nothing. Harris dragged his desk chair across the carpet once again and pointed at the smoke alarm, nodding at Rhys. He watched as Rhys got up on the chair. 'Unscrew the lid,' he instructed. Rhys did so.

'What is— Oh, shit ... is that what I think it is?'

'I think so,' said Harris.

'Where? But why? Who?'

'Get down off there,' said Harris, 'and follow me.'

A few minutes later in Raphael's room, Rhys was starting work on the laptop. 'I should be able to break it,' he said. 'I'm going to need my laptop from the car. Two secs.' He ran back out and returned with his MacBook and a bundle of wires. He plugged them in and then spent the next ten minutes going between the two computers, typing various things into each while Harris looked on. Then he said 'Bingo.'

He sat back and Harris saw the desktop screen of

Raphael's laptop. 'If I'm right, there'll be some sort of remote camera software,' Harris said. 'But I suppose it might be difficult to find.'

'Oh, come on, this is child's play,' said Rhys, and within less than a minute he'd found a programme called ReCord Security Plus. 'I've got the destination folders. Ah, they're password-protected, of course, but if I just… Ha, thought so. Same password as before. So if I just— Woah.' Rhys stopped, staring at the screen.

'What?' asked Harris.

'There are a lot of files. They seem to be organised into different folders marked One, Two and Three. One and Two have a lot in them. Three has only two files.'

'What's in Folder One?' Harris asked. Rhys clicked on them and opened up the first. It was a video file and the footage instantly filled the screen. It showed Harris in his bedroom, his back to the camera, pulling off his top.

'Holy fuck, this guy has hundreds of these,' Rhys said, 'he's been editing them down to bitesize highlights. He's one crazy fuck.' A quick swipe through the other videos in the folder showed they were all the same. Harris getting out of bed or walking back into his room from the shower. 'He's fucking obsessed with you,' Rhys said, shaking his head.

He then navigated to Folder Two and picked one of the files at random. At first it looked to be more of the same, with Harris unbuttoning his jeans. Then he realised there was more to this video as it became obvious what Harris was doing.

'Okaaaay,' said Rhys. 'I don't know whether to laugh or be mortified for you, mate.' He swapped to another video in the folder, which showed Harris sitting at his desk with something playing on his laptop, leaning back on his chair, his jeans around his ankles. 'Certainly spotting a theme to this folder,' said Rhys. He flicked to the next. The same again, this time with Harris stretched out naked on the bed, one hand behind his head, the other very much occupied.

'Fucking hell,' Harris said, 'I can't believe he's categorised them all.'

'Interesting technique,' Rhys said, tilting his head. 'I mean, I'm a left-handed guy, too, but that's … creative.'

'Oh, shut up,' Harris said. 'Go to Folder Three. Although I think I have a pretty good idea what it will be.'

'I'm intrigued. Are you sure you're okay with me seeing?' Rhys asked.

'I think that ship's well and truly sailed,' Harris said, letting out a resigned sigh. 'Just press play.'

Rhys navigated to the third folder and played the first video. Sure enough, it confirmed Harris's suspicions. It featured him kissing and fumbling on the bed with a young woman.

'Who's that?' Rhys asked, just as the woman pulled off her top. 'Woahhh who is *that*?'

'A sister of one of Raphael's uni friends. They all stayed over. She ... um ... got the wrong room during the night. I invited her to stay.'

Rhys let out a low whistle. 'You can be a smooth fucker, I'll give you that.'

'I think we should stop that one there while she's still got her knickers on,' said Harris. 'No need to look at the other video in there. I know what it will be.'

'If she's anything like this one here, I think we should take a look,' said Rhys, grinning.

'The next one will be a guy I met on Tinder.'

Rhys skipped to the one remaining file and froze the image as soon as it came on the screen. It showed Harris and another man, a little older, standing in the room, talking.

'Is there a place where the raw, unedited content goes? Like, before Raphael's had a chance to snip and categorise it?'

'Yeah, sure, it's here,' Rhys said. 'Looks like a few days' worth of recordings.'

'He's been at Lauren's,' Harris said. 'Can't have had time.'

'And there's a bin, too, where he must ditch all the unused stuff, said Rhys. 'That's empty. I could try to resurrect anything that's gone if you want?'

'No need, I just wanted to know two things. First, is it possible to find the part where I discovered the camera and snip it out?'

Rhys was flicking through the video footage. 'Yeah, should be easy – I think the camera must be motion-triggered, so it will just look like you went into your room at a later time. I doubt he'd figure it out. I could just remove all of today's if you want?'

'No,' said Harris quickly. 'No, he knows I'm at home. That would be suspicious. And this afternoon is important.'

'Why?'

'Because of what I got up to this afternoon.'

He raised his eyebrows at Rhys. He eventually got it. 'Oh, the gardener lad?'

Harris nodded. 'I presume it picked it up?'

Rhys dragged the slider along the video footage then let it play. 'Yep. Here you are. Shagging your little heart out,' he said matter-of-factly. 'You sure you wouldn't prefer I just binned all this?'

'No. It's important we keep it on there. It needs to be there and we need to allow Raphael to view it, decide to keep it, and then file it away into his sick little folders. Folder Three, presumably.'

'Right,' Rhys said. 'I mean, yeah, that's all fine, but why? I mean, you could just delete everything, or confront him? All this is probably illegal, surely?'

Harris stayed silent for a moment, thinking. Then Rhys added, 'And perhaps … I don't know … perhaps you should tell Lauren about this.'

'Lauren?' Harris frowned, confused.

'Er … yeah. Surely she'd be interested to know that her soon-to-be-husband is, like, crazily obsessed, perhaps full-blown in-love with, his adopted brother. And it's even more fucked up when you consider you're actually brothers. Even without the slightly incestuous shit, I think she'd probably want to know that her husband likes guys. It's not fair on her to keep it secret.'

Harris shook his head. 'I don't really care about Lauren.'

Rhys frowned. 'That's … kind of cold, isn't it?'

Harris ignored that. Thinking of Lauren as a person within herself wasn't something he'd really done up until now and he didn't feel this was the time to start. That would distract him from the ideas that were forming. He felt a buzz he hadn't felt before, although he thought he'd got an essence of it when he'd expressed his anger and frustration in the empty house in Essex a few days before. 'You know I said I needed a plan? Proper nuclear-level impact? Well, I think I've got it.'

Chapter Thirty-Two

HARRIS

The day of the party

Harris has gone over every part of the plan in his head. Every part he and Rhys have masterminded. And the parts Rhys knows nothing about. The parts that nobody can know anything about. Not until it happens. Not until he rolls the dice and sees where it lands. He knows there's room for error. Too soon and his plan will be ruined. Or at least not as effective. Too late and there's a chance he might be stopped before he's said everything he wants to say. Although he likes the idea of a neat, perfectly executed plan, he has to think of this as a bit of a shot in the dark. A leap into the unknown. A chance to have it all come together, but a situation where he'd have to be adaptable. See if it works and go with whatever happens.

Over the past months, he has pushed back on Rhys's attempts to make him abandon the whole thing. He'd occasionally tried to remind Harris that Raphael was likely guilty of some crime or other with the covert camera and he could easily call the whole thing off and bring down the family that way. But Harris wouldn't be swayed. So Rhys has helped him put together the file that will be used to override Raphael and Lauren's desired content on the TV screens at the engagement party. Content that will shame the whole family. 'Don't you want to get justice for what he did to your mum?' Harris asked Rhys on a particularly tense night, as Rhys stared at him from his computer, doubt in his eyes.

'Of course,' he'd said, quietly.

'Then everyone needs to know what Patrick Moncrieff is like. Not just his son, not just his wife. He needs to be named and everyone needs to know why.'

Now that it's nearly time, Harris gazes over at Rhys, who is standing in his waiter's uniform. If only he knew what was to come. Knew the lengths Harris would go to. Both their futures are in the balance tonight. He finds that exciting, but he knows that if Rhys is fully aware of what is going on here he won't feel the same.

The first part goes well. Smoother than he'd hoped as he intercepts a circular tray of drinks. Makes sure they are taken to the head table where Patrick, Isabelle, Raphael and Lauren are sitting. Lauren's parents take their seats a little later and he's pleased to see they still have full glasses. They are a complication he hasn't considered, but it seems a crisis has been averted.

'Stop fussing with the champagne and sit down,' Isabelle hisses at him. He does as he's told. Just as Patrick stands up to give the first speech. Harris sees the guests finishing their conversations. Some tapping their neighbours on the shoulder, telling them that the speeches are beginning. Young women, around the same age as Lauren, brushing their hair back behind their shoulders, smiles wide. Groups of handsome young men in blazers and pastel shirts, some wearing sunglasses. Harris recognises a few of them as Raphael's university friends. Guys who he'd seen slap him on the back. Say 'Congrats, mate.' They seem genuinely happy for him, albeit in their rather smug, self-satisfied way. Harris wonders how they'll feel in less than an hour's time. Less than half an hour. Twenty-minutes perhaps. Because when it starts, it won't take long for this sparkling, picture-perfect world to come crashing down.

'Ladies and gentlemen, friends and family,' Patrick begins. 'Thank you so much to everyone who has travelled to our home today to celebrate the engagement of my son Raphael to the lovely Lauren. Of course, this set-up would normally happen at the actual wedding, but these two young lovers have decided they want a small private ceremony on holiday later this year without fuss, so have decided to mix these things up, as young people like to do these days, and have this gathering today in lieu of a traditional wedding reception.'

Harris looks over at Lauren's parents. Neither look very happy. He wonders if anyone at the garden party has sussed out for themselves that the whole pregnancy thing is the reason the engagement is being held now, and not when Lauren will obviously be too pregnant. He turns his gaze to Lauren, her happy, smiling face. How much of it is real happiness, he wonders, and how much of that is for the guests. He's always got the sense she's the more committed one in the relationship – that she'd want to be marrying Raphael even if she wasn't pregnant. Her expression is certainly more enthusiastic than his. He has his polite, tight-lipped smile on. Ready for the outside world, but perhaps paddling hard underneath, Harris thinks. Whatever they're actually feeling, he's very aware those smiles will be nowhere to be seen very soon.

For a moment, he gets lost in imagining an alternate future. A future where Lauren and Raphael are off playing happy families, when Patrick and Isabelle are doing their best to play happy grandparents, and Harris is once again on the sidelines – an awkward secret manifested, a shard of glass in their side who just won't go away. Destined to be resented, dismissed, ignored. Or used and then discarded whenever it suits them. That is how this family works. He doesn't imagine it changing just because one of them now has a ring on his finger and a new wife by his side.

'...and we are overjoyed,' continues Patrick, holding a hand out to gesture to Lauren, 'that our family is going from three to four with the addition of a charming daughter-in-law.'

Smiles, nods, a few 'Ahhs'. Harris feels sick.

Even Lauren gets an official name. *Daughter-in-law.* Whereas he's always been the hard-to-define one. The issue. The 'Oh-he's-someone-we've-taken-in' orphan who the family would rather not have to explain. He feels a rage course through him, and if he'd had any doubts about what he is doing, what is about to happen, they are extinguished in a moment. He doesn't care if they put him in handcuffs and throw away the key. It will be worth it. For him. For his mother. For everyone who thinks the Moncrieffs are a perfect family.

Patrick has just finished a toast to Raphael and Lauren when the latter leaps up and tells everyone that, whilst it may not be traditional for the bride-to-be to make a speech, she very much wants to say a few things. 'It is on a day like this when you realise how truly blessed one is to live in this world and with the people who make it glow with sunlight and cause the birds to sing.' If he wasn't so nervous, Harris would be scoffing at this. He notices a few raised eyebrows and hears Great

Aunt Elda say in a carrying murmur, 'Is she a hippie or just cracked?'

The rest of Lauren's speech is the usual thanks to her parents and 'dearest Raphy's parents'. Harris isn't mentioned. The whole thing ends with another toast, then Lauren sits back down, and looks pointedly at her fiancé, clearly hoping Raphael will leap up to echo her feelings.

But before he can, Harris rises to his feet.

'I'd like to say a few words,' he says.

'Oh, of course,' says Lauren.

'What? No, Harris, sit down,' Raphael says through clenched teeth.

Isabelle joins in. 'Harris, I'm not sure this is part of—'

'The plan? Sure it is?' Harris cuts her off, grinning at everyone. Isabelle, halfway to her feet, smiles round as if to reassure people. He sees her turn to look at her husband, then back at him. And as she does so, a hazy distant look appears on her face.

'*Sit down*,' Raphael mouths at him.

'No, no, *Raphy*,' Harris says in an overly affectionate tone, smiling at him. 'I just want to add my thanks and share some good wishes. I know how modest you are and don't like people championing your qualities in public, but I think it would be impossible to say too many nice things about you and your lovely wife-to-be, am I right, ladies and gentlemen?' He looks at the guests. Some of them have raised eyebrows, a little perplexed, but most are smiling and laughing and making general sounds of agreement.

'Well,' Harris says, taking out his phone. 'As I said, I just wanted to add my thanks to Lauren's already very thorough speech. Although, of course, Lauren's speech didn't mention me at all, and neither did my father's— Sorry, I mean *Patrick*'s.'

He taps his phone and the two screens – one to the left and the other to the right – change to a photograph. A photograph that makes Patrick rise abruptly from his seat. And then instantly fall back down.

'Calm down, Patrick, I know this isn't your best shot, but you were a handsome young man.' Some guests laugh as they stare good naturedly as the photo of Patrick. It was from just under twenty years ago. Harris had found the photo in an album in the library and taken a scan of it. 'When you think about it you look vaguely like your charming older son here, Raphael. But the eyes – they're not dissimilar to someone else's. Green eyes. Like mine.' He touches his phone and the photograph changes to an image of a woman. Laughing. On a beach. 'This is my mother.' He glances over at Patrick and can see the photograph's had an effect – he looks stricken. Horrified. But he doesn't move. Harris carries on. 'My mother was having an affair with a handsome man she briefly worked with. She and my dad became family friends with the Moncrieffs, particularly Patrick. During this *friendship*, she became pregnant. And so a baby with the same piercing green eyes was born. Me.'

The audience is no longer a mass of smiling faces. Murmurs and whispers have broken out. The Moncrieffs remain completely still in their chairs. Just as Harris had hoped.

'I wasn't the only child, though. There is another, though at his request, I haven't included his face on these screens. His mother kept him secret from the controlling, abusive man she had been sleeping with. But he exists. And so do I. We are both children of a careless man.'

Harris looks at Patrick. A blank expression meets him, but he thinks he can spot fear and horror in the man's eyes. He must be losing his sense of movement now, Harris thinks, otherwise he'd be making attempts to stop him. All he's able to do now is just sit and listen.

'Well after that bombshell, and while we're on the subject of sons,' continues Harris, tapping his phone once more, 'let's get to the man of the hour. Raphael Moncrieff.' The screens change again, this time to a grinning picture of Raphael that has been swiped off Instagram. 'And brace yourselves, everyone,' says Harris. 'In the words of a TV continuity announcer, the following content contains scenes some viewers may find … disturbing.'

Chapter Thirty-Three

HARRIS

The day of the party

Harris clears his throat, ready for what is to come. 'Raphael has always been such a supportive big brother. In case you don't know the whole tragic back story, I'm the kid this lovely, kind, *caring* family took in when my parents died in a car accident. As I said, my mum and dad were friends of the Moncrieffs, although we'll interrogate that relationship more closely shortly. Anyway, I was taken in by them and dearest Raphy here was the life raft I needed. Warm and generous and supportive. Like, really hand-on-heart supportive. You know what I mean.' Harris takes a breath, feeling a lurch of nerves and excitement. 'So supportive, that he seduced me during my first year living in this house.' Harris thinks he hears a very prominent gasp somewhere to his left and is pretty sure it's Lauren's mother, although he doesn't turn to look at her. 'Afterwards – well, the morning after the night before, as people say, when he was ashamed and confused about what had transpired between us – he blackmailed me into helping him with his school work. As I said, *so* kind and supportive. A model son. A model student. And what big brother doesn't like to keep tabs on his little brother, eh?' He taps his phone. The image on the two screens either side of them changes once again. An image fills the screen. A moving image.

'This is me in my bedroom. And that's me, as you can see,' Harris says, nodding to the screen on his left. The video footage did indeed show Harris removing clothes, slinging them onto his bed. When he turned around, with his front facing the camera, a pixelated line appeared that followed him across the screen that said 'CENSORED'. 'This is from a small hidden camera I found in my bedroom,' Harris says. 'The smoke alarm had been adapted to have a surveillance camera within it. Pretty neat technology. That's how much Raphael *cares*. He just needs to know what I'm up to.' The screen changes to another clip – and the content of it causes audible gasps. 'I know. It's shocking. Such an invasion of privacy. Raphael has *a lot* of these, saved in a helpful little playlist. Really convenient for him, and this one,' the video changes again, 'is me and a young lady – a woman he knows, actually. A friend of a friend. Don't worry, she's not here today, I checked. I wouldn't do that to her. But it's important to see the sort of lengths Raphael will go to in order to keep me safe.' Out of his peripheral vision he can see the two moving figures on the screen. 'I'd just like to say, unless there's any room for doubt, that CENSORED line on the screen has been added on – I just didn't want you all to have to see everything, I do value my privacy – Raphael, on the other hand doesn't do *censored*. He likes to see everything that's happening. He's just that caring. Needs to know it all.' He allows himself a smirk. 'Admittedly, Raphy here didn't actually know it was his *half-brother* he was covertly watching all this time. Didn't actually know that he had inadvertently committed incest either. But at least he does now. And so do all of you.'

He hears Lauren's father mutter, 'Jesus fucking Christ.' This makes Harris smile even wider. He had wondered if the shock of the video would cause someone to intervene, to stop him on his quest to tell everyone the truth. But it seems that the guests are transfixed. Eyes wide. Mouths even wider. In the brief moment it takes him to scan the crowd, he thinks he might see delight and amusement in their eyes. Hunger, even. Perhaps some of them hate this family, too. Resent them. Maybe envy them. Ready to revel in their downfall. Eager to hear what he has to say next. He won't disappoint them.

'And last but not least, we get to the wife,' Harris says, tapping his phone again so a new image floods the screens. 'Of course, the woman you see pictured here isn't Isabelle Moncrieff. This is an actor. Natasha Crewe. You might've seen her in films.' The footage plays a clip from an action movie, then another from a romance – Natasha leaning in to kiss her male co-star. 'Now, you see, Ms Crewe is often the object of desire in her films and matched with men older than her forty years of age. She'll hate me for announcing her age to everyone, she likes to pretend she's younger. That's often how it is in Hollywood. In real life, however, Natasha likes ... the younger man. Boys, in other words.' The screen now shows a photo of Natasha at a film premiere. To the left, in the background, it's possible to make out Isabelle talking to someone. 'Isabelle has been responsible for casting Natasha in a couple of recent films for a well-known film studio. To do this, she took me out to America and left me at Natasha's mansion unaccompanied. I was, essentially, a gift for Natasha. A gift she could do what she wanted with. Now, again, I'm going to be fair. I did have sex with her of my own accord. In the moment, I rather enjoyed the experience. But like I said to her earlier today when I reminded her of this, it really doesn't sound very good, does it? Me, a seventeen-year-old boy handed over as a gift to this older woman. Rather inappropriate, wouldn't you say? But then it's thrown into entirely new territory when you consider the drugs.' Harris taps the phone and two photos, taken from Google Images, replace the film premiere image. Two pill bottles. Side by side. 'Just in case you can't make out the words, the one on the right says Diazepam, often referred to as Valium, and the one on the left says Oxycodone Hydrochloride, sometimes referred to as OxyContin. Now, I don't know which of these drugs Ms Crewe decided to put in my strawberry lemonade – my money's on the Diazepam, looking back at how my afternoon panned out, but it could have been either. And drugging teenagers to make the seduction a bit easier isn't a good look for a Hollywood star. Or the person who went along with it.' He looks pointedly at Isabelle. Like the other two members of her family, she was sitting completely still, staring forward, not moving.

'So ladies and gentlemen, there you have my happy family, The Moncrieffs,' he says, holding out a hand to gesture over to them, as if they are a new product line and this a retailer convention. The guests have turned to stare at the completely frozen family, unsure what to think or do next. The silence is palpable. After what seems like a never-ending pause, a crash echoes around the marquee. Patrick has slumped forward, knocking his glass over, wine spilling across the crisp white tablecloth. His head hangs against his chest, the pose painfully unnatural.

'He's having a heart attack!' someone shouts.

'It's a stroke,' another says.

'Call an ambulance!'

'Help him!'

The guests are realising en masse that something terrible is happening. Not just a social scandal involving shocking but oh-so-juicy details about the awful things the Moncrieffs have been up to. This is no longer a gossip-fuelled fall from grace. This is the stuff of life and death. People start to rush towards the family. Lauren's state of silent horror has given way to panic. She shakes Raphael at her side but he isn't moving. 'Raph, your father. Get up, help him!' But no matter how much she shoves his shoulder, he stares blankly into the distance, as does Isabelle. Lauren's mother has now come round to the front of the table, trying to help their daughter wake her fiancé.

Raphael's making a noise now. A terrible noise, just about audible above the noise of the commotion. A steady, drawn-out whine. A noise of illness. A noise of pain. A noise of desperation. 'Oh, God. Oh, God,' cries Lauren as Raphael continues to make the awful sound. All the while, Patrick and Isabelle make no sound at all, something that the guests seem unsure whether to consider a good sign or an indication of something worse. Lauren's father says something about checking their airways. A young woman – perhaps one of Lauren's friends – shouts recommendations ranging from 'the recovery position' to 'chest compressions'. Waiters and catering staff stand around looking lost and helpless as people lift and shake and check the pulses of each of the Moncrieffs. Anything on the tables around them is swept aside, smashed on the grass, trampled underfoot. Elderly couples look on worried, others try to get to the front, to be in on the action, to help save the day. One of the younger guests, a bored-looking girl of around twelve or thirteen, in a pink dress and matching trainers, stands somewhere near the edge of the throng, to the left of one of the screens, calmly filming the whole thing on her iPhone, presumably to post to social media. It may well be the most interesting thing she's ever witnessed first-hand, and still she needs to view it through the prism of a backlit screen and a camera lens.

It's the girl filming it that makes Harris force himself to stay present and focus. He definitely doesn't need to be caught on camera. It's time to leave. Harris finds Rhys's face across the crowd. His expression had been blank but is steadily turning to concern. For a moment, Harris thinks he's going to go over to the Moncrieffs, but then he sees Rhys heading towards him.

'What's wrong with them?' Rhys asks urgently as he reaches Harris.

'Time to go,' Harris says, pulling him along.

'What?' Rhys says, confused, but finds himself dragged along behind Harris.

Harris allows himself one last look back before turning away and striding forward. In that snapshot glance, he sees the bride-to-be shaking her fiancé, trying to get a response, his blank eyes are vacant, his body limp. No words form on his lips.

As he and Rhys walk away Harris hears the commotion, the panic rising, the guests unsure what to do now their hosts have been incapacitated.

'Phone an ambulance!' someone shouts again.

'I have, they're on the way,' says another.

'Give them space, give them some air!'

The chaos becomes more distant as Harris leads the way around the side of the house.

'Where are you going?' Rhys asks.

'Away,' Harris says. 'And you're coming, too.'

'Am I?' Rhys asks. 'Because whatever happened back there – that wasn't part of the plan.'

Harris rounds on him, not hiding the glee in his eyes, the buzzing euphoria inside him.

'It was always part of the plan,' he says. 'They're getting exactly what they deserve.'

Chapter Thirty-Four

HARRIS

The day of the party

'We need to help them,' said Rhys as Harris marches up to the car.

Harris ignores him. He tries the door of Rhys's car but it's locked. He then turns and walks up close to him.

'What are you doing?' Rhys asks, stepping back. Again, Harris sees fear in his eyes. Rhys is scared of him.

Harris reaches into Rhys's left-hand pocket and pulls out the car keys.

'You can't drive, you're not on the insurance,' Rhys says.

'Watch me.'

'This is all wrong, Harris,' Rhys says, his voice strained, filling with panic. 'You weren't supposed to drug them. The speech and presentation was going to be enough.'

'How did you think it was going to play out? That they'd just sit there and let me carry on? One of them would have pulled the plug or physically stopped me. I just made sure that didn't happen.'

'What did you give them?'

'Just a little something in their wine glasses. Don't worry, it will wear off. It looks more dramatic than it is. Now, let's go.'

While Harris opens the driver's door. Rhys is clearly teetering on the edge of a decision. He looks back through the trees towards the grounds of the Moncrieff's home. Then he walks round the car to the passenger door.

'Fine. I'm coming.' He drops himself into the passenger seat as Harris starts the engine and accelerates hard, speeding down the drive and turning the corner onto a side road, way too fast.

'Christ, slow down,' Rhys says. 'If you get pulled over by the police we'll both be in trouble.'

Harris lets out a low laugh. 'I think speeding's the least of my worries right now. But, God, today was worth it. The looks on everyone's faces. Did you see them?'

'Yeah,' says Rhys, 'but … I don't know. I'm not sure what I think about the whole thing now.'

'Oh, come on, you were brilliant. That presentation was expertly put together, it couldn't have come off any smoother. And now everyone knows all their sick secrets, everything they've done. They're poisonous. Poisonous, the lot of them.'

'And yet you're the one who poisoned them,' says Rhys, a note of aggression in his voice.

'Yeah. There's a touch of poetic justice about that, don't you think?' says Harris, turning to grin at Rhys. But his brother isn't grinning back.

'No. It's twisted. I'm not sure why I went along with it all.'

'You know what that man did to your mum. Just dumped her when he was finished using her.'

'I know,' says Rhys. 'But what you did doesn't change any of that. And who are you to judge?'

'What's that supposed to mean?' Harris snaps, weaving dangerously around a slower car ahead of him.

'Well, all your talk about Isabelle and that actress. How are you any better than either of them?'

'Christ, you've lost me,' Harris says.

'Well, you took the gardener's son up to your room and screwed him, didn't you? Knowing the entire thing was being filmed just so you had something on Raphael, which, as it turned out, was entirely unnecessary, since he had a lot of similar shit saved already.'

'I don't see what your point—'

'The boy was around the same age as you were when Isabelle took you to Natasha's house. How are *you* much different to her?'

'I didn't fucking *drug* him. I didn't—'

'And you know what? I'm not sure if today was really focused on your special revenge plan or if it was just an opportunity for you to have the fucking limelight for a change. Getting to do your big speech. You loved it, didn't you? Everyone gasping while your family watched on, unable to move because of whatever shit you'd poisoned them with.'

'They're *not* my family,' Harris snaps.

'They're all you've got,' Rhys says.

'We've got each other!' Harris shouts. 'You and me. We're leaving and we're never coming back, okay? I've got your passport in my bag.'

Rhys stares at him in astonishment. 'What? You're mad. You're actually insane.'

'You're just saying that because you're always too scared to actually take any action,' Harris says, turning the wheel too quickly on a bend and scraping the side of the car along an overhanging hedge. He puts his foot down on the accelerator, hurtling down the winding country lane.

'Harris, it isn't too late. Stop the car, turn around and go back to the party and tell the paramedics what you gave them and then go with them to the hospital.'

Harris says nothing, just continues to push the little KA faster and faster.

'Harris!' Rhys yells.

'The paramedics won't be able to save them.'

Harris glances at Rhys's face after he says this. He can't resist a smirk at the shocked look on his face. The dawning comprehension.

'You … you're not serious…'

Harris shrugs. 'Why not? What possible good do they add to the world?'

'I … you said … you said they'd be completely fine, that they'd all be okay.'

'Not sure I worded it quite that way, but granted, I just needed you to shut the fuck up and stop delaying us.'

'I can't believe this,' Rhys says, his breathing quickening, sounding as though he is about to have a panic attack. 'Stop the car.'

'No.'

'Stop the fucking car, you fucking psychopath.'

Rhys lunges forward and grabs the wheel, just as Harris is navigating a sharp corner.

Neither of them see the slow-moving vehicle around the other side of the bend. At least, not until a split second before their car collides with it head-on. Harris vaguely registers it as a tractor, but everything goes black after that.

Sounds. Voices. Dimly he hears a voice close to his ear, someone bending down next to him. He drifts in and out of consciousness, unsure how much time has passed.

'What's that?' someone says.

Another says, 'His wallet.'

There's some shuffling.

'Pick it up. We can use it to get in touch with his family.'

Chapter Thirty-Five

HARRIS

After the party

Harris barely speaks to the medics who treat him. He's unnerved and confused. Can't stop flicking his eyes over to the young man in the chair in his hospital room. It hurts every time he moves his head, so he can only really see part of him. But he recognises the brogues, the trousers, the cardigan-clad arm. Occasionally he speaks. He sounds concerned and caring and Harris hears him tell the staff there's no way Harris is up to speaking to the police.

Then, when they're alone, he comes up close to the bed, moving his chair along the ground. The scraping sound causes Harris actual physical pain, but he doesn't mention it. He just wants to know what's going on.

'How are you doing?' he asks. His voice is natural. Harris isn't sure what to think. Unsure what to answer.

'Water,' he eventually gasps.

He hears liquid being poured into a cup. It's raised to his lips. He sees Raphael offering him a small smile as he gently allows Harris to take a few sips. He even dabs his lips with a tissue.

'So, how are you doing?' he asks again.

'Awful,' Harris croaks. 'I feel like I died.'

'You almost did,' he says. 'Not sure if this is sad news for you or not, but your pal Rhys didn't pull through. In fact, I think they said he died on impact.'

'My half-brother,' Harris murmurs.

'What?'

Harris coughs. 'He wasn't a pal. He was my half-brother. *Our* half-brother.'

Raphael sighs. 'Well, so you say. I just thought you'd like to know. I very nearly died, in case you were wondering. Well, I'm not convinced it was a close-run thing, or if you just didn't have the heart to kill me, too.'

Harris says nothing.

'You do realise they're dead. Mum and Dad. Oh, yes. I presume you intended that to happen. Or did you just accidentally put too much in their drinks? Either way, you could still go to prison. They're going to interview you. As soon as you're well enough.'

All this information makes his head hurt. He tries to process it all, but it's like a brick wall has been built around certain parts of his mind – his memories, his feelings, some of them are being kept away from him. A protective instinct, possibly.

'Although I think they've started out on the wrong foot, so to speak. I'm no detective, but I can spot some errors being made already. They seem to think that your accomplice was actually the mastermind.'

This revelation hits home for Harris.

His back-up plan is working. The moment he started to guess that Rhys wasn't entirely on board with his plans, he'd made some careful decisions. Made sure Rhys's laptop was the one he used to do the pharmaceutical research. That it was Rhys's fingerprints on the drugs stored in the glove compartment of Rhys's car. That he'd have a prime opportunity, as a waiter at the event, to poison the wine.

'Figures,' Harris says, quietly.

'So did you mess up my dosage? Or did you mean to kill me too?' Raphael sits on the end of the bed, facing him.

Harris just stares at him.

'Okay, don't tell me. I don't even want to know. I'm just interested in what happens now.'

Harris continues to stare at his brother.

'You're probably wondering why I'm not devastated my parents are dead. Well, not that you've ever really cared what I thought, Harris, but I fucking hated them, too. You did me a favour. Now I get ... well ...

everything. And I'll take care of you.' He lays a hand again on Harris's arm.

'I know why you're doing this,' Harris says, each word causing him pain, but he forces them out. Raphael raises his eyebrows.

'You're doing this because of the videos.'

He pulls his arm back. 'Yes, you got the wrong end of the stick with that.'

'I don't think so. It's one thing to have a covert camera constantly recording an adult without their knowledge. But it's another to have footage of underage teenagers having sex.'

A tension becomes visible in Raphael's face, but he is clearly trying to remain calm.

'If that boy was underage, then you've committed a crime, too,' Raphael says, his voice now icy.

'But he wasn't underage.' With supreme effort in spite of his pain, Harris explains. 'The age of consent in the UK is sixteen. But when it comes to photos or video, you have to be over eighteen. And even then, believe me, it's best that they actually *know* that you're keeping them stored on a fucking laptop. There's a whole library of criminality on that hard drive, but that particular video is the killer, I think. And you might be able to navigate the social shame I unleashed upon you, make excuses, say it's all made up. But it's something a lot harder to deny when there's cold, hard evidence. And the shame I'm sure you feel now considering you know, well, that I'm your little brother.'

Raphael holds his gaze. 'What makes you think I haven't destroyed all the evidence.'

Harris smiles, the muscles in his face protesting, but it's worth it seeing the panic in Raphael's eyes. 'What makes you think I haven't already taken a copy?'

They continue to look at each other. 'I get the feeling this is heading to a deal.'

'I get the feeling it is, too,' says Harris.

'In the end, everything's a transaction,' says Raphael.

'I take it the wedding's off?'

'Lauren is taking some time to think about what she wants,' Raphael says. 'It's a lot to process. But then, so is the amount I'm set to inherit so ... let's say she's conflicted. But I know Lauren. She's tough. Tougher than she looks. Good at brazening things out. And she likes nice things. Things that cost money. I dare say she'll come to the right decision.'

'You actually want to marry her, then?'

Raphael shrugs. 'I've decided a respectable marriage could be the best thing for me right now. Patch over the difficulties of the past. The optics are better if we settle down as husband and wife. A happy family.'

'Just like your parents did?' Harris rolls his eyes then studies Rapheal for a second. 'So ... you want to know that I won't say anything about you if *you* don't tell the police about me?'

Raphael confirms with a short nod.

'Fuck,' Harris says, 'you're a colder fucker than I thought.'

'There's something else – well, two things.'

Harris lets out a heavy breath. He is growing tired. He needs to sleep. But he also knows he needs to finish this conversation.

'I'll lie for you. Say I saw that Rhys boy spiking the drinks or whatever might help. We can iron that out. I just want to be the one to care for you.'

Harris frowns. 'What?'

Raphael puts a hand on Harris's leg. 'I want to help you with your recovery. Help you wash, help you dress. I'll care for you, Harris. You'll stay in the main house to start with, then, once you're able, you can live in the annex. It will be nice, having you so close. And there will be money. Regular top-ups of cash. You'll never want for anything.' He leans forward, an intensity now burning in his eyes, an excitement in his face that Harris hasn't seen before.

Harris thinks about all the times he's seen Raphael watching him. Looking at him. The camera. The videos. 'Christ, you really are obsessed with me,' Harris mutters. 'I'm … I'm your brother.'

'Half-brother.'

'It's really fucked up.'

'When has this family been anything else?' Raphael says, allowing a smile to start to show.

Harris suddenly feels an urge to laugh. But it's accompanied by a wave of nausea, so he fights it. Then he asks, 'What's the other thing?'

'Sorry?'

'You said there were two things you wanted from me. What's the second one?'

'Oh,' Raphael says, pulling his hand back and getting up off the bed, moving towards the door. 'Just one little thing.'

'What?' Harris asks, not sure what to expect.

'I need you to finish my final-year coursework.' He flashes his best Raphael Moncrieff grin. 'Just give it a read through and make some edits. I've always been so appreciative of your help.'

Epilogue

Six months after the party

Harris has been comfortable in the little annex. Well, 'little' is a relative word. 'Little' compared to the main house. But still quite a large property. He's made it his own, bought things with the allowance Raphael pays into his account on a regular basis. But over the past months, he's been alarmed at how small the amount of money has become. And late in arriving, too.

After Harris had been deemed fit to leave hospital, Raphael had been very attentive. Just as he'd said he would be. He helped him dress, shower, get into bed. He'd visit multiple times a day. They didn't talk much and Harris didn't try to initiate conversation. He knew why Raphael was there. He wanted to watch him. To look at him. Then go back to the house and wrestle with the guilt and confusion of it all – or so Harris presumed.

But it seemed that guilt and confusion had grown too much of a burden. The visits went down to once a day, then once every other day. Then once a week. As Harris's injuries healed and he became more able again, Raphael seemed to suffer an internal crisis. Perhaps he felt the pretence of it all being about Harris's care could no longer be maintained. Maybe it just got too much for him to bear. Maybe Lauren was asking too many questions or her resolve was finally wavering. There were a lot of questions and Harris didn't know the answers. Initially, the payments arrived on the first of the month. That was the agreement. But as the months have gone on, it's become later and later. Harris has had to pay a visit to the main house to remind Raphael of his obligation.

This has happened more than once. On one occasion, Raphael was having a dinner party with his friends. He was clearly tipsy and became aggressive towards Harris, saying he wasn't invited. Harris recognised a few of the guests. His university friends. Some of them had been at the engagement party. They hadn't all abandoned him, it seemed. 'Nice to see you all again,' Harris had said, grinning at them.

Lauren had jumped up, trying to smooth things over, first inviting Harris to stay for a drink, then, when Raphael objected, ushering Harris out of the door telling him to go back to his home.

'Sorry to be the debt collector, Raphy, but you're late again,' Harris called out to the dinner table as Lauren half steered, half pushed him into the hallway.

'He'll sort it,' Lauren said, 'now just go, please.'

Harris looked at her, stared into her eyes. 'How do you stand it?' he asked in a quiet voice. 'Why do you pretend?'

Then a cry came from upstairs. A baby's cry.

'I think you've got your answer,' she said, quietly, a tightness in her face making her look older than her years. 'Now if you'll excuse me, I'm going up to assist the nanny with getting little Willow off to sleep. Good excuse to leave that lot,' she'd added, with a smile. Then she'd left Harris in the hallway, walking up the stairs, not turning back.

On one of the other occasions when he had to remind Raphael of their payment agreement, he had found his half-brother sitting by the swimming pool, drunk. So drunk, he was unable to string his words together, lolling back on his sun lounger in the darkness of the evening. Things were becoming difficult.

Time moved on.

Harris's comfortable existence gradually felt less stable. The days when Raphael had helped Harris with his recuperation began to feel like a distant memory. He had expected Raphael's incestuous obsession with him to increase as part of their tense agreement with each other, but that hadn't occurred. An awkwardness between them had been clear from the start and by the time Harris had been ready to move to the annex, his half-brother could barely meet his gaze. He had expected to become Raphael's pet. Instead, he'd become his curse. A reminder of the things he was most ashamed of.

To an extent, the ongoing issues with Raphael provide Harris with something to focus on. Allow him to push his conflicted feelings deeper down. Feelings of guilt. Regret, even. They are never all-encompassing, they never take over his mind and tear at his soul. But they are there, floating around inside him. The scale of his betrayal towards his other half-brother. A boy who, in death, has been painted in the public eye as a disturbed murderer, while Harris endures suspicion without punishment. Without the evidence, CPS thresholds can't be met. Charges can't be brought. There isn't much anyone can do.

Some months have now gone by without any money at all. He hasn't spent everything Raphael has given him, but it makes him worry. Worry what the future holds. He'd taken a year off from university after everything that happened. His course supervisors had been nothing but understanding. It felt like a stable plan. It had even been approved by Raphael, provided he always came back to the annex during the holidays. Providing Harris was there for him and his secret desires. But now those desires had dwindled and the financial security ahead of him seems less certain.

So when Lauren comes to visit him, he wonders with trepidation what twist his story is going to take next.

'Can we talk?' she asks.

He nods and shows her through to the living room. He asks if she wants a tea or coffee, or something stronger. She declines, so Harris doesn't bother to get one for himself. They sit on the sofas.

'You've made this place look nice,' she says, 'a lot of cream and warm-beige.'

'That wasn't me. It was painted like this already,' Harris says.

'It's strange to think I've never properly been in here,' she muses.

Harris doesn't know what to say to this, so he says nothing.

'I'm here because we have a problem.'

Harris frowns. 'I'm guessing this is about your husband?'

She nods. 'Yes, it is. He's ... struggling.'

'Financially?' asks Harris. 'Is that why he's late in his payments.'

Lauren sighs. 'Harris, may I give you some advice. If you're intent on this life of blackmail you've carved out for yourself, perhaps think of a more sophisticated way to talk about it. That little outburst at the dinner party back in the spring, all guns blazing *where-is-my-money* – that was the opposite of classy. And you rather incriminated yourself, too.'

Harris can't help but laugh. 'Look, in all honesty, Lauren, I don't know how much you know, how much Raphael has told you and whatever understanding you have going on with him, but after everything that's happened, I'm not sure you have a leg to stand on when it comes to judging what's *classy*. Most other women would have left him.'

She leans forward suddenly, looking more earnest than she has before. 'How long do you think this can last, Harris? I'm not saying I know every detail about what occurred, and quite frankly I don't want to know, but as far as I understand, your little blackmail operation isn't as clean as you would like to think.'

Harris looks back at her. He feels his pulse quickening. He has the feeling he's at one of those turning points where the picture shifts and a new path forward becomes visible.

'Why are you here, Lauren?' he asks.

She looks at the floor for a few seconds, her mouth pinched, as though she were biting her tongue. Then she says, 'If Raphael and I divorce within a certain period of time, I don't … get much.'

Harris shrugs. 'You could challenge that in court.'

Lauren nods. 'I could…' she says, slowly. 'But there are … other options.'

Harris raises an eyebrow. 'Other options?'

Lauren still has her eyes on the carpet. 'His drinking … and the way he is with me… He's … well, he's actually rather horrible these days.'

'I'm sorry to hear this,' Harris says.

Lauren nods sadly.

'Can I ask, just … hypothetically,' Harris says, leaning forwards in his chair, 'what happens if … if he was to die before you.'

Lauren doesn't answer for a moment, then she says, 'That would work out much better for me in many respects. Much … cleaner. But it's unlikely such a tragedy would occur. Unless…'

'Unless?' Harris prompts.

'Unless one day, his drinking became so bad, he went for an inadvisable night-time swim.'

Harris watches her. She's still not looking at him. But he gets the feeling they're very much reaching the heart of the matter here. The reason for her visit.

'I've seen him out there,' Harris says, nodding. 'In the evenings, sometimes. Empty bottle by his lounger. Sometimes asleep in the centre of the pool on an inflatable. It's … an accident waiting to happen.'

Lauren's eyes come up from the floor now. She looks

Harris in the eyes and he sees the resolve in there. A hardness he's never given her credit for. 'It is.'

They look at each other for a moment. Then she says 'Of course, if such an accident were to occur, I couldn't be involved. I'd have to be … away, somewhere. With Willow. I can't cope with mess, you see. And Raphy does leave the place in a bit of a state. I like things to be neat and tidy. Better off things were … done and dusted, while I was off-stage, so to speak. But in the end a bit of mess can lead to a much tidier resolution. Almost like a sort-out. A detox. Do you see what I'm saying? And I'd be so grateful to whoever happened to be on-site, looking out of the window of the annex, here, who managed to pull my Raphy out of the water. Even if they were a little too late to actually save him. The effort wouldn't go … unrewarded.'

Harris leans back. 'I see.'

Lauren smiles. Then she rises from the sofa and says, 'Well, I must get back inside. Can't stay here chatting all night.' Suddenly, she's back to the jolly, normal Lauren. The one who beams her way through life and is lightness and kindness to everyone she meets. Providing her life remains neat and tidy.

'I'll be planning a trip with Willow soon. I'll take her to stay at my parents' place in Islington for a week. See some friends, do some shopping. I'll pop back before then, though. So we can … make some plans?'

Harris nods.

'Good,' she says, beaming. 'I'll see myself out. I'm sure you have a lot to think about.'

Indeed he did, Harris thought as Lauren closed the door quietly. He watched as she walked across the lawn back to the main house. Indeed he did.

Acknowledgments

I'd like to say a huge thanks to all the readers who have picked up my books and taken the time to recommend them to friends, leave reviews online and post about them on social media. I'll always be extremely grateful.

Special thanks to my family: Leno, for continued kindness and encouragement throughout the writing process, my parents, sisters Molly and Amy, granny and uncle, and to Rebecca and Tom and all my close friends.

I would like to thank my wonderful agent Joanna Swainson and everyone at Hardman & Swainson for being such a brilliant team. Huge thanks to my editor Jennie Rothwell and to Kimberley Young, Charlotte Ledger, Bonnie Macleod, Emma Petfield, Lucy Bennett, Arsalan Isa, Chloe Cummings and everyone at One More Chapter and HarperCollins. I'm overjoyed to be part of an amazing publisher family. Thanks to Lizzy Barber, Fiona Cummins, Simon Masters, Lauren North, Marion Todd and Michael Wood for all the wonderful WhatsApp chats during our writing days, along with joyful lunch trips! Massive thanks to the authors who so generously read early proofs of this book (with a really tight turnaround!) and offered such kind words.

Last but not least, a big thank you to all the booksellers who have been so brilliant at getting my novels into the hands of readers.

Everyone is capable of murder. Are you?

It started with an invitation to dinner. An evening of good food and good company at a luxury villa. But as the night progresses, the party takes a dark turn.

The host makes you an offer, a party favour he calls it: another guest has committed a heinous crime, you can end their life, stop their terror. He tells you there will be no consequences; do you believe him?

Your decision will change your life. Choose carefully.

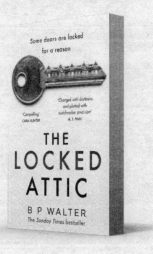

There's something in my neighbour's attic.

Something steeped in shadows. A secret to everyone.
Seen by no one…

He stands sometimes at the window. Hidden in the
corner of my eye.

I know he's there. I know he's watching.

Now my son is dead. My neighbour is not.

And I'm going to find out why.

Two strangers meet on the pier
Only one walks away...

Screenwriter Caroline Byrne is desperate to know why
her daughter Jessica died, murdered in Stratford when
she was supposed to be at a friend's in Somerset.

When Caroline discovers the messages Jessica had been
sending a boy named Michael, she realises it's because of
him. Because he failed to meet her that day. He's the
reason why her daughter is dead. And so she makes a
choice. He's the one who's going to pay.

That is her promise. Her price.

**Four people walked into the dining room that night.
One would never leave.**

Matthew: the perfect husband.
Titus: the perfect son.
Charlie: the perfect illusion.
Rachel: the perfect stranger.

Charlie didn't want her at the book club. Matthew
wouldn't listen. And that's how Charlie finds himself
slumped beside his husband's body, their son sitting
silently at the dinner table, while Rachel calls 999, the
bloody knife still gripped in her hand.

**If you go down to the woods today,
you're in for a big surprise...**

Kitty Marchland has always known that her family aren't like others. But when her father uproots them to a remote cottage in the woods, she realises that her parents are keeping secrets from her – secrets that could unravel everything.

Years later, Kitty starts to question what really happened out in the forest. When the police revisit a suspicious death, she must examine her most painful memories – and this time, there's nowhere to hide...

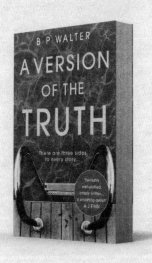

We all see what we want to see...

2019: Julianne is preparing a family dinner when her son comes to show her something on his iPad – something that will make her question everything about her marriage and turn her husband into a stranger.

1990: A fresher student at Oxford, Holly is well out of her depth when she falls into an uneasy friendship with a group of older students and begins to develop feelings for one in particular. He's confident, quiet, attractive, and seems to like her too. But she soon begins to realise she might just be a disposable pawn in a very sinister game.

YOUR NUMBER ONE STOP

ONE MORE CHAPTER

FOR PAGETURNING BOOKS

The author and One More Chapter would like to thank everyone who contributed to the publication of this story...

Analytics
Abigail Fryer
Maria Osa

Audio
Fionnuala Barrett
Ciara Briggs

Contracts
Sasha Duszynska
Lewis

Design
Lucy Bennett
Fiona Greenway
Liane Payne
Dean Russell

Digital Sales
Hannah Lismore
Emily Scorer

Editorial
Kate Elton
Arsalan Isa
Charlotte Ledger
Bonnie Macleod
Jennie Rothwell
Caroline Scott-
Bowden
Emily Thomas

Harper360
Emily Gerbner
Jean Marie Kelly
emma sullivan
Sophia Wilhelm

International Sales
Peter Borcsok
Bethan Moore

Marketing & Publicity
Chloe Cummings
Emma Petfield

Operations
Melissa Okusanya
Hannah Stamp

Production
Emily Chan
Denis Manson
Simon Moore
Francesca Tuzzeo

Rights
Rachel McCarron
Hany Sheikh
Mohamed
Zoe Shine

The HarperCollins Distribution Team

The HarperCollins Finance & Royalties Team

The HarperCollins Legal Team

The HarperCollins Technology Team

Trade Marketing
Ben Hurd

UK Sales
Laura Carpenter
Isabel Coburn
Jay Cochrane
Sabina Lewis
Holly Martin
Erin White
Harriet Williams
Leah Woods

And every other essential link in the chain from delivery drivers to booksellers to librarians and beyond!

ONE MORE CHAPTER

YOUR NUMBER ONE STOP

FOR PAGETURNING BOOKS

One More Chapter is an
award-winning global
division of HarperCollins.

Subscribe to our newsletter to get our
latest eBook deals and stay up to date
with all our new releases!

signup.harpercollins.co.uk/
join/signup-omc

Meet the team at
www.onemorechapter.com

Follow us!

 @OneMoreChapter_

 @OneMoreChapter

@onemorechapterhc

Do you write unputdownable fiction?
We love to hear from new voices.
Find out how to submit your novel at
www.onemorechapter.com/submissions